STAR-SPANGLED SWAGGER

SEDUCTION IN RED, WHITE & BLUE

KAMYRA HARDING

Star-Spangled Swagger – Seduction In Red, White, and Blue

Copyright © 2024 Try Hard Mommy

TryHardMommy.com

KAMYRA

Note from the Publisher: This is a work of fiction. Any resemblance to actual historical events, persons living or dead or references to locations, persons, events, or locations is purely coincidental and used fictitiously. Other names, characters, circumstances, places and events are imaginative and not intended to reflect real events.

Cover Designed by IBDesignz by Iesha Bree www.ibdesignz.com

Edited by V. Rena of Red Diamond Editing reddiamondediting5@yahoo.com

SYNOPSIS

Amara, a determined professional from New York, finds herself at a crossroads in her career and considering a new job. As she prepares for the next phase of her life, she is suddenly faced with unexpected feelings for Jordan, a proud Atlantan who has always known what he wants - Amara.

After being apart for seven years, Amara and Jordan cross paths again during a 4th of July race in Atlanta. As they revisit old feelings of resentment and attraction, they realize that life can change in just one day. Will they abandon their plans and give in to their feelings? And even if they do, will the distance between New York and Atlanta keep them apart?

FOREWORD

KAMYRA

Thank you so much for choosing this book! I'm excited to introduce you to Amara and Jordan. Their story unfolds over the course of one day, and I can't wait for you to join them on this journey. This book is the result of my adventure with the Just Write Collaborative, where we were tasked with creating a story centered around the Fourth of July. It was definitely a challenge to tell a complete tale in just one day, relying heavily on dialogue. However, it also was an opportunity to demonstrate how long conversations can be the perfect prelude to romance. Life-changing moments may occur in just one day, but often, we only realize it in retrospect as they unfold naturally, like a beautiful blossoming flower.

PROLOGUE
JANUARY

J ordan read the article more times than he could count. That didn't stop him from skimming it one more time. He skimmed words he'd committed to memory weeks ago and zoomed in on the headshot - again. Amara Shaw, Vice President and Senior Program Officer of Peace and Security for the Mutatio Foundation, was gorgeous. She had been beautiful during their school days but now was stunning.

She'd worked her way up from a program assistant position in the Civic Engagement Division, which she secured when they graduated from The New School. While climbing the Mutatio ladder in Manhattan, she managed to earn a doctorate as a full-time student at the University of Southern California. A native New Yorker, Amara attended Columbia University before The New School and USC primarily online. There wasn't mention of a spouse or children but plenty of references to articles she'd penned and her funding strategy. She was a 30-year-old phenom in philanthropy. She served on the board of a youth track program in Brooklyn and numerous other organizations, but the profile had nothing about her interests or hobbies. It existed strictly a career piece.

Jordan recalled another recently read local news article listing the Mutatio Foundation as a lead sponsor of the Sweet Tea Independence Day Race. He remembered it because Mutatio required all its senior staff to attend the event, and Amara was the youngest senior staff member. That meant she was coming to Atlanta in July. And, if she didn't have a spouse to mention in the profile, she might be coming alone, or better still, she was single. Jordan wanted her to be single for a few reasons. Selfishly, he liked the idea of her being a viable option.

He had a thing for her in school, and the profile piece picture reminded him of a latent desire to know whether the skin on the her body looked as flawless as that of her face. The memory of graduate student Amara haunted him. He'd never gotten her out of his system. She slipped in without fanfare and stayed hidden, waiting to resurface. Selflessly, he wanted her free of her fiancé. The annoying prick didn't deserve her.

Nine years ago, 27-year-old graduate student Jordan Harris found himself at a party his fraternity hosted in an underground Manhattan restaurant turned club for the night. The beats were live. The women were plenty. The crowded room smelled like grenadine, grain alcohol, and sweat. The scene was everything after weeks of nothing besides accounting and nonprofit management classes. He stood at the bar, setting things in motion with a shortie, when he saw a couple going at it on the opposite side of the room. He kept looking because they were doing more than the usual bump and grind.

*The woman was cute and petite. Her full, brassy weave obscured the man's face. He stood at about six feet with a solid medium build. The pair shuffled and turned to the beat of the music. That's when Jordan saw the man's face. He recognized the dude with a carefree, self-assured, almost smug expression. Jordan swore to himself. The guy was engaged to his classmate Amara, **not** the woman who'd just* *retrieved her tongue from down dude's throat. Immediately, Jordan regretted leaving his cozy Morningside Heights studio. Amara was cool people, and ol' boy was out here cheating on her in full view of God, the Devil, and everyone. When the couple unraveled from one another, Jordan seized the opportunity to pounce. He aggressively approached the bar, closed the distance between them, and tapped the man on the shoulder.*

"Hey. I'm Jordan. We met at Zeke's birthday celebration. I'm in Amara's program." Letting the man know that Jordan knew him and to whom he belonged.

"Whasup? I'm Erwin." He slapped Jordan on the back without detection of guilt. "Yeah, I remember." His brow furrowed as he looked me in the eyes and growled, "You frat?"

Jordan slowly nodded in Erwin's direction, a lackluster move followed by a scowl. He knew what that meant. Erwin was reminding him that frat loyalty preceded all others. Jordan may have caught Erwin cheating on Amara, but he couldn't do anything about it. Frat allegiance dictated he held his tongue, something Erwin hadn't been doing. That wasn't the last time he witnessed Erwin's dirt. He hated being a small part of the deception. Guilt plagued him. Usually, he wouldn't care, but this included **Amara Shaw***, the woman for whom he'd gladly forsake all others. She was smart, good looking, and ambitious, with a sly sense of humor that bordered on quirky.*

Before this incident, he thought her pairing with Erwin odd. Now, he didn't understand at all. Jordan thought she was too young to be betrothed to anyone. But wasn't that how suckas got the good ones? They swept in when the women were too young and innocent to know better than to tie themselves to fully grown boys who'd never become men. Amara deserved a **real** *man. Though he played it off well, the culpability made him uncomfortable around her. After a while, her energy changed. Not only had she stopped being pleasant, but she was nearly hostile towards him. He didn't know whether she knew that he knew about Erwin's wandering or what. It was for the best. He didn't* *need the drama. He stayed far from her and did his two-year bid in the master's program and New York City without incident.*

"Cool. Next round's on me."

"Naw. I've got to get back to my company." Those were the last words Jordan ever spoke to Erwin. Whenever they bumped into one another, with or without Amara, Erwin spoke and offered to buy drinks. Jordan always nodded, grunted, and declined.

1

AMARA

JULY FOURTH

I'd never been one to celebrate the Fourth of July. After I outgrew marveling at fireworks, I realized it was just another excuse for cookouts and a day off. Don't get me wrong. I loved a good cookout, especially with banging music. But I didn't need a federal holiday to enjoy it. One sanctioned day didn't make the ribs more tender or the line dancing more fun. But, in one day, your entire world can change. That's precisely what happened to me. At 5 a.m. on the Fourth of July, I stood on a street corner in Atlanta, Georgia, being jostled by 60,000 of my closest friends. Compulsively looking around and through the crowd, I tried to find one person, when my earbuds announced, **"Call from Taneka."** They should have said, "Girl, hold on to your athletic bra straps," because that call set things in motion.

"What do you mean where am I? I'm on the corner where we agreed to meet. Where are you? I'm looking around. I don't see you. What color are you wearing?" I was beyond frustrated with my best friend, and the sun had yet to announce itself to the day.

"I'm at home." She sounded rough, like she'd been gargling coffee beans instead of drinking their juice. I barely heard her through the loosely organized chaos around me. I needed her to repeat what she'd sighed. She couldn't have admitted to not leaving her house. If she were still there, she wouldn't make it on time. I must have misheard her.

"Say again. Speak up."

"I'm in bed. I stayed up past my bedtime last night. I'm not coming."

"What do you mean you're not coming?"

"I did too much *cumming* last night. I can't walk nine miles in the o'dark early. I barely got to my car last night. Or this morning?"

"You what? With whom? We were together last night. You dropped me off and went home."

"I dropped you off. I did not go home, at least not to my house. I texted my mechanic. He fit me in for a tune-up."

I couldn't believe her. Of all the irresponsible things, we're girls. I was frustrated, annoyed, and curious. "A tune-up? How old are you? You reached way back for that one."

"Listen, I'm a luxury machine requiring specialized servicing. Vern handles me just right."

"Vern, the mechanic, seriously?"

"Stop hating. I got mine, and now I need my beauty rest. You should try it. Lord knows what's under your hood. The poor thing probably is rusted shut. A man would need a crowbar to pry it open."

"I can't with you."

"Go. Run your little race. I would've just held you back. Now you can run with the other former track superstars instead of being in the back with me. Go relive your college glory days." Even in sarcastic fun alluding to my time running track for Columbia University was a low blow. She knew I considered that one of the best times of my life.

"Taneka, come on! Are you kidding me? I got up—you know

what? You're right. I'm going to find my wave. I don't have time for your foolishness. This race is about to begin. There are helluva people out here. I don't even know which direction to go. I'm just going to follow the crowd. Bye."

I don't know why I wasted my energy being upset. Taneka was always trifling. She also was fun and got me out of what she called my serious crab shell. In college, she perpetually dragged me to trendy clubs that young and dumb Amara had no business stepping into, especially in the skyscraper heels and bodycon dresses she insisted I wore. By the night's end, those shoes had my feet pulsating in pain. Campus parties were more than enough for my sneakerhead, bookish tail. But Ms. Thang imagined herself too good for college boys. She wanted to meet a rich husband in a New York City club. She dreamed of parading him around Southwest Atlanta, taunting the mean girls who made high school hell for her. Taneka was one of those people who came into their own during college. What had been chubby morphed into deliciously thick. Since she couldn't dump the glasses, she became an optometrist with her own line of eyeglass frames. She turned everything that made her unpopular in high school to her advantage. Her penchant for hair pieces, weaves, and wigs meant you never knew what you were getting when you saw her. She's the one who got me into the braid styles I wore throughout school.

I loved my girl, but her oversexed ass had me rushing through thousands of barely dressed runners looking for the elite starting wave. It's a good thing I wanted to run in the Sweet Tea Independence Day Race; otherwise, I would've been banging on her front door instead of dodging through the thick crowd.

Unlike flakey Taneka, the crack of dawn race time didn't bother me. I was used to being awake before sunrise, exercising, and preparing for the day ahead. I wasn't used to delicately pushing through throngs of people, trying to get to my starting place at the front with the rest of the elite runners, those who ran fast and were significantly along the route before the end of the pack crossed the starting line. Usually, I arrived at races well ahead of the start time. But no, I'd agreed to a later start and to wait for Taneka towards the rear, in her slower starting wave. All that courtesy got me was evil stares as I nudged people, excusing myself while jogging up the moonlit avenue towards the sound of an announcer rattling off sponsors and race instructions.

After slipping under the rope blocking Wave A from the rest of the pack, I went into autopilot mode. My comfort zone was stretching and deep breathing at a race starting line. I'd been here numerous times. The musty smell of nervous perspiration emanating from runners on both sides of me was as familiar as rice and peas cooking in my parents' kitchen. Tens of thousands of jittery bodies bobbed up and down to the pulse rhythm echoing in my ears. There was an authentic, fun race vibe. In front of me, a tall Jimmy Walker lookalike wore Uncle Sam booty shorts and had the nerve to do toe touches two inches from my face. By the time the race began, I felt intimately acquainted with his backside. Other racers wore American flag capes, socks, shorts, hats, and whatever else they found with the Stars and Stripes. I could tell I was in for a good time. Without Taneka to distract me I cued up an audible book and had to keep increasing the volume to hear it over the loud crowd. People were jazzed about the race in a manner I'd never experienced before. It felt intoxicating, and we hadn't even begun.

The corniest announcer's voice was heard through huge speakers strategically placed near every other race wave. He bordered on irritation, except people seemed to enjoy his 1973 pop radio disc jockey cadence and yelling.

"Ladies and Gentlemen, this is what you've been training for... nine miles of sightseeing in Hot'lanta, the Peachtree City in the hills. Check your laces and brace for those hills. I see you,

Betsey Ross. Don't drink too much beer at mile three. You could lose your wig. Before we begin, let's thank the race organizers and sponsors, without whom you wouldn't suffer in this heat. Speaking of sponsors, here's a shout-out to Sweet Tea of Atlanta. Thank you for bringing us this race each Fourth of July. What's your favorite flavor? Don't say peach. That's too easy. I like the spiced watermelon sweet tea and, of course, classic sweet tea. How about you? Yell out your favorite. Do it loud enough for them to hear in the corporate headquarters down the street. The tea may be sweet, but your sweat won't be at the end of those nine miles. Good luck with that. Kidding. You've got it. See you at the finish line. Racers, take your marks. Let's do this!"

Usually, I'd roll my eyes at the cringy announcer, but that day, I didn't. He kind of reminded me of my dad. He had a sense of humor tailor-made for himself, others be damned. He'd double over belly laugh at his own jokes while the rest of us dissected them, searching for the humor. Well, all of us except my mother. She loved his jokes. If soul mates were real, they had to be them.

Booooom!

Instead of a horn, the starting signal sounded like a cannon; probably a nod to the American Revolution. I sprinted three paces ahead of booty shorts Uncle Sam, the next closest runner. Blocking everything out, except the road in front, I'd forgotten about Taneka and the life-changing call I'd been praying to get. Chasing a runner's high was just the mind cleanser I needed, feeling the tension rolling off my back. For fifteen kilometers, all I had to do was keep putting one foot in front of the other and listen to a book that I hadn't had time to read.

With every step, my feet sunk into the memory foam of my over priced, high-performance running shoe. Even though the sun barely peaked its dome, my moisture wicking tank was already sticking to me as sweat slowly dripped down my back. It reminded me of the time in college when the runner to my left at the starters' block mocked me for perspiring before the gun sounded. She wasn't so cheeky when I smoked her and the rest of the line. I may sweat like a pig, but I run like a cheetah. That's why I wasn't as upset with Taneka as I made her think. Without her, I could actually *run* this famous race. We agreed that I'd walk it with her while we caught up. Without her holding me back, I could go full speed and burn off tension from waiting to hear if I got the job of my dreams.

The last time I was this excited about a new job, someone stole it from me. Maybe not stole, but I deserved it more than the person who got the offer. This time, no one could edge me out. I'd spent the past three years working six, sometimes seven days a week and finishing my doctorate so that I'd be ready for the next golden opportunity. Yep, I definitely needed a destressing run through Atlanta alongside a few thousand equally damp, fast people.

I ran along the left flank, the fast lane to pull out of the crowd. I cut left, excusing myself and pointing toward the sidewalk where onlookers were cheering runners, holding signs, and ringing cowbells. My strategy was to get past the DJ booth to pull ahead in the dead zone. While listening to my book, I started thinking about my happiness. *I'm due something good. I need a break from being reliable, Amara. A few days off, away from home and my responsibilities, will do me some good. It seems like I haven't had fun since Erwin left. Between school and work, I haven't had time for fun. I pledge to reclaim my life beginning today.*

We were a quarter of a mile into the nine-mile race when I jogged diagonally toward the street's left side. As I crossed in front of a group of women dressed in matching red, white, and blue tutus, in my peripheral, I saw one runner cut off another, causing him to trip and lose balance. It must have been too dark to see everything because it appeared as if the first guy purposely shoved the second, who stumbled directly in front of me. One moment, I was in the zone. The next, a couple of Titans were barreling towards me. They were a blur of black, white, and powder blue. The one who wore a white tank and Adidas running shorts with sewn-in black compression tights hurtled over the other's back as said back careened toward the ground in my path. Luckily, my quick reflexes enabled me to sidestep him and barely miss being crushed. The first guy kept running as if nothing happened. I'd witnessed a skip and run. The victim twisted his ankle and hit the ground hard, landing on his right hip. Around us, people were rubbernecking but didn't stop. I managed to sidestep him before he came crashing down to the steaming asphalt. People ran around him, shaking their heads.

As much as I wanted to keep going, I couldn't. Jerry Johnson, the best middle school track coach ever, always told us humanity overrode wins. That's why I sacrificed my race time to help the fallen soldier, or in this case, weekend warrior. Good thing I did because he was rolling back and forth, clutching his left ankle. I reached my hand down to him, thinking I'd pull him over to the side and get a volunteer to call a med team. It took all I had to pull his dead weight to a sitting position. That must have been why I hadn't gotten a good look at him.

"Thanks," hissed a silky baritone. I knew *that* voice. It was from my past. Recognition dawned on him at the same time it did for me. We spoke at the same time.

"Amara?"

"Jordan? Here. Let me help you." I extended my hands crossed at the forearm for stability. He had at least 50 pounds on me. It looked good on him —even as he sat helpless on the ground, rocking side to side like a self-soothing baby. We managed to get him almost standing. He leaned into me.

How did he smell so good during a race? He didn't smell like any cologne I knew. If it were his natural pheromones, that would be proof that God played favorites. The man was tall, at least

6′2″. I didn't remember him being built like a professional athlete. I could feel muscles pulsating beneath his powder blue tank top. The color looked gorgeous against his lickable caramel skin. *Lickable? Where did that come from?* Sure, he's the color of my favorite Sees's butterscotch lollypops, but he wasn't syrupy candy.

"Naw, I'm good." Jordan pushed himself up off of the road but winced when his left foot touched down. "Ouch. Maybe you can spot me while I hop over to the sidewalk."

He appeared to be in a lot of pain and I couldn't leave him to suffer. "Are you okay? Let me take a look."

"You a doc now?" If he weren't trying to get rid of me, I'd think he and that cute smirk were flirting. Silly thought; Jordan Harris would never flirt with me.

"No, but I do know about running injuries. Sit on the curb while I test your ankle."

"It's good. I think I can walk it off." He hesitantly took a few of steps and ended up plopping his lengthy body on the curb, biting his bottom lip, and massaging that ankle.

"Walk it off? Really?" Men and their machismo. Why couldn't he accept help? "Fine. I'll travel with you for a bit."

"I'm good. Go on."

"I can't. You know the proverb. I saved your life; now I'm responsible for it."

"You're absolved. There are medic tents along the route. I'll stop at one." He limped away, careful not to put weight on his left foot. He was having a hard time balancing with runners dodging around him, knocking him this way and that. He wouldn't get far without help or risk further injuring himself. I couldn't let that happen.

"I'll accompany you just in case." I don't know why I offered to walk with him. In the past, I vowed to keep Jordan as far from my orbit as possible. Buddy-walking with him in the Sweet Tea was the opposite of that. Nothing good would come from this.

The man radiated danger. I'd have to dump him in a medic tent or ditch him as soon as he could hoof it alone, whichever came first. Jordan Harris, with his perfectly arched thick brows and dark brown, two-inch twists sprouting from his crown, was not my business. Plus, I hadn't stopped fuming from what he did back in school. *Were those natural highlights in his hair?* He had the nerve to look like an older version of Kelly Oubre Jr. I didn't know much about basketball, but I did know fine. In the dictionary, next to the word was a picture of Jordan Harris. *Stop staring, Mara.*

We wandered in silence, taking in the carnivalesque scene surrounding us. I thought about the difference between this race and others I'd run. The Sweet Tea wasn't just a race—it was more than that. This year, the largest 15-kilometer race in the world attracted people from over 64 countries. Some ran, others walked, and more lined the route, partying and cheering from the side-walk as we trekked through the street. I attended because my foundation sponsored it at the highest level.

I hadn't ever seen a race like the Sweet Tea. Running was a serious endeavor for me. Growing up, I enjoyed competitive running. Later, it became a mental and physical wellness tool. I approached it as warmly as I did, taking nutritional supplements and drinking three liters of water daily. This wasn't serious. The Sweet Tea had DJs every few blocks, people distributing food and alcoholic drinks, water sprays, and costumed participants. Most people walked or jogged with their phones, took selfies, and recorded sights. Buildings were decorated for the holiday. I didn't know there were so many Fourth of July decorations. Children were cheering and waving pinwheels as runners passed. It was unorthodox and exactly what I needed.

As we approached the one-mile marker, I saw a line to take selfies with the red, white, and blue sign, definitely unconventional. I assumed the Wave A runners didn't do that. By now, they were far ahead of us. I decided I might as well enjoy the sights until I could separate from Jordan. With him shuffling beside me, I remembered Taneka. "Excuse me. I need to send a text." I tapped out a quick message.

> Amara: Hey, Girl, this will take longer than I thought. I literally ran into a friend from The New School. We're walking together.

Buzz. Buzz.

"Please tell me it's a man," Taneka barked as soon as I picked up the call. I waved, signaling Jordan to ramble ahead so he couldn't overhear my loud friend.

"Hello to you too, Taneka Jane Watson."

"Stop using my whole government name. Who are you walking with, and is he fine?" She always got right to the point. Crazy as she seemed, Taneka was a genuine friend who wanted the best for me. She embodied the fun ying to my serious yang.

"You don't know it's a –" She interrupted me before I could distract her.

"Please. You wouldn't jeopardize your race time for a woman. Spill it. Spill the sweet tea. See what I did there?" No need to deny it; I shook my head and confessed.

"It's Jordan, " I whispered.

"The Jordan? As in, *the man* who had you going to confession even though you weren't Catholic? The star of your wet dreams, Jordan? The, if only Erwin were a bit more like that, Jordan?"

"I regret that bottle of tequila. Or should I call it truth serum?" During spring break of my first year at the New School, we vacationed in Punta Cana in the Dominican Republic. Taneka studied optometry at Emory then. Miraculously, our breaks coincided. We soaked up the sun, splurged on spa services, and did a lot of nothing; until Taneka decided to reproduce our favorite pool swim-up bar drink. Her idea was sound. We'd save a lot of money by making and bringing drinks to the beach. The wrench in the plan was drinking the whole batch in one night of sister bonding.

I'd forgotten most of that night. I do recall that we were smart enough to keep our drunk selves on the private beach-view balcony attached to our room. I hadn't had tequila since. Everyone had that one spirit, a reckless time ruined for you. Tequila reigned supreme for me.

"Tequila Sunrise Margaritas are the bomb, and you know it. Answer me, bitty. Are you talking about *that* Jordan?"

I assumed an excessively cheery voice, "Yes. I can't talk. I'm busy walking the race you flaked on. I'll let you know when I'm in route to your place."

"Okay, okay answer this. How was it when you first saw him again after all this time?"

"T, I felt all the things when I first saw him."

"All the things?"

"Yes! All... the... things!"

"Girl, you had better not abandon that man for me. Get yours."

"Hangin' up, bye." I tucked my phone into the zippered back pocket of my tank top.

Taneka was right. I noticed Jordan more than an engaged woman should have. In my defense, all of the single, straight women, gay men and fluid persons in the program were after him. I didn't recall him dating any of them. Although, I'd caught him noticing me a few times. It was weird. Out of nowhere, I'd get a warm, sweet, almost orgasmic sensation; I discretely **scanned** around, and sure enough, he'd be staring at me. I always looked away, but it would be too late. He saw that I saw. He never turned his head nor did he ever approach me about anything except schoolwork.

Satan was busy one semester when we were paired on a team

project. Late nights strategizing and writing pushed my libido to an all-time high. Poor Erwin unknowingly benefitted from Jordan's influence. I knew it was wrong to jump my fiancé because I lusted after another man, but a woman had to work things out. Eventually, I went into overdrive to complete the project alone. Thus, limiting our time together. He angrily called me a control freak but went with it once he confirmed the quality of the product. Despite the fuss, he didn't appear too mad watching me do my part of the client presentation. If I remember correctly, he seemed downright proud and a tad enamored. Probably wishful thinking, but I recalled it like that; a man who checked most of the proverbial boxes appreciated me.

If I hadn't been engaged, I still wouldn't have considered Jordan a viable romantic option. The whole time we were in the program he adamantly insisted he'd return to Atlanta the day after graduation. That city had nothing for me. I've always been a *'til I die* New Yorker. Except, was I?

Trekking alongside Jordan as he increased weight on his ankle, I got lost in thoughts. Maybe walking instead of running was for the best. Instead of ignoring it, I needed to talk myself through the decision. I wanted the job. It encapsulated everything I wanted professionally. I wasn't blind to my life being little more than work. I knew what I was missing. Getting this job would make previous sacrifices worth everything I'd missed. I still had time to do things. But it would be sweeter if I did them as president of the newly formed Ngero Foundation. The entity's creators were already proposing impactful work, and they hadn't opened the doors.

As the first president, I'd decide where and what type of impact. I'd assemble a committed, knowledgeable team of experts and service delivery professionals. The thought of it gave me goosebumps. The team I'd assemble would empower people to craft their change. We'd listen to them, finding ways to fit the foundation in as a solutions-finding partner. The best part was that the astounding budget. Money wasn't everything, but it was necessary, and Ngero planned to apply it to help solve world issues. I wasn't worried as much about getting the gig as about what that meant since Ngero headquarters were in Atlanta.

Feeling overwhelmed, I cleared my mind of all stressors. In the moment, I pledged to enjoy a walk with an intriguing man, have fun, and continue with life. Based on his current speed, I could manage that for a couple of hours.

2

JORDAN

Damn if he didn't bodycheck me. Not how this was supposed to happen. My embarrassment multiplied when I saw Amara Grace Shaw leaning over, staring as if I was a problem to solve. The wicked witch of grad school, one I had a thing for, although she hadn't always been mean, and she was the best-looking witch, saw me face plant on the asphalt.

As she spotted me while I tested my ankle, I got a good whiff of her. Among funky people on a hot morning, the woman smelled like lavender, vanilla, and home. I knew because I had a thing for lavender. Maybe this hadn't been a brilliant idea after all. *Focus, Jay.*

"No braids." I bork the silence with a statement, not a question. In graduate school, she'd worn her hair in any braid style that piqued her interest. I always thought she resembled a taller version of Janelle Monae. Wondered whether they were related. Both had beautiful, flawless, deep brown complexions. It fascinated me that, like Monae, Amara's hair should have been a Museum of Modern Art installation. Back then, I low-key wanted to play in it. Talk to her about how she decided which style to sport. I knew it wasn't as simple whimsy. Nothing about Amara connotated whimsical. She was one of those people who transversed the earth with intention. The kind who made others think they knew life's secret meaning.

I loved her hairdos. Styling her crown was Amara's most noticeable form of creative expression. For a creature of habit, her revolving coifs were a mystery. Her wardrobe didn't mirror her artsy hair. Most days, she wore athleisure and high-end loungewear clothing. But her hair was a character like Isa Rae's in *Insecure*. Each style appeared tailor-made for her features. When deep in thought, she fingered a long braid she'd pulled around from the nape of her neck as if stroking it helped her concentrate. A few times in class, she caught me watching her coil her fingers in a braid, working them up and down.

Today she's working this cute 'fro, though. Instead of a trendy itty bitty the slightly longer afro highlighted her natural curls. What am I doing? Three seconds in her presence, and I'm obsessing again. It's ridiculous. I ought to be thinking about how my kids at the center I run will roast me. I'll never live down a wipeout in the first mile. I shouldn't have hit the ground like that. Shit felt like being hit by a Falcons' defensive tackle. I have to finish this race to prove to them that we can do hard things. I want to show them that everyone struggles sometimes, but exceptional people keep going.

I signed up to prove I could meet a challenge to the kids. Hoping that me doing something this challenging would inspire them. The plan was to use this stunt to encourage them to identify a personal challenge, draft a strategy to meet it, and then share it with the group. They'd be accountability partners. Together, the students would learn they could overcome obstacles and have first-hand knowledge of the power of a solid support system. That was one of my goals for today.

Amara twisted the gold knot earring in her left ear. "You remember that? I needed a change, out with the old and all that.

After graduation, life got hectic. I cut my hair to streamline my morning routine." Her voice baptized me in a smooth, velvety timbre. It nearly hypnotized me. She spoke just loud enough to force you to pay attention and with enough authority that you feared missing something important. I barely heard it when she was on the phone. That phone call she took could have been a man since she quickly sought to take it in private. I couldn't hear a word but I wondered if it had been Erwin.

The alum newsletter piece merely omitted a husband. It didn't go further. I was so excited that I forgot she still could have been engaged. She didn't have a ring on today. That was a good sign, or not; most runners didn't wear them during races. Swollen fingers made rings uncomfortable and impossible to remove.

Get it together, Jay. It's like you stepped out of a time machine set for seven years ago. I'm back to thinking about someone who didn't care about me when she saw me every day and certainly forgot about me the day after graduation. I don't lack female company, yet here I am, wondering about a woman who barely knows I exist. I blame that damn article. She wasn't on my mind until it hit my inbox. Doesn't matter because I'm stuck on the Amara train. I want to ride her 'til to the last stop. Riding her... Shit. Stop. Let me chill and see what type of vibe she's emitting.

Determined to push past the awkwardness, I tried again, "So, what have you been up to for the past seven years?" Thankfully, the corny line led to conversation.

She did that thing people do when they don't want to talk but are too polite to ignore you. They give you short responses, daring you to dig deeper. "Working and finishing school." Her curt reply contrasted with the compassionate look she gave my ankle. Apparently, taking care of me didn't include talking. Good thing I wasn't easily deterred.

"Finishing?" I prompted while swerving to avoid colliding

with an expensive looking, black infant running stroller. What I didn't need was to fall again in front of her.

"After the New School, I got a doctorate in organizational change and leadership from USC."

Pretend you don't know. "Look at you. So, you are a doc?"

Her mouth curved upwards into a sly smile. Was she wearing lip gloss? If I didn't know better, I'd have accused her of teasing me. "I am. I did that while working full-time at the Mutatio Foundation. I managed to work my way up to VP and Senior Program Officer of Peace and Security." I learned this from her profile in our alum newsletter but played like I didn't so she wouldn't know I'd been harmlessly stalking her for longer than I'd ever admit. "And you?"

This wasn't the time to talk about myself. I needed to learn more about her. "Still working at the community center. What else have you been doing?"

"That's it. School and work took all of my time. Now is my season to reap the benefits of that sacrifice."

"OK now, I hear you. What are you planning?"

"The usual, travel, hobbies, and spend more time with loved ones." She pointed ahead to an elevated DJ booth surrounded by racers. "Are they doing YMCA? Oh, I'm getting in on that." Without glancing back, she jogged to the crowd. I did my best to keep up. My felt tender, but it didn't bother me enough to lose her in the crowd.

Being slower had its perks. I admired the view. Amara's tight ass and thighs barely jiggled in her tiny black running shorts. They weren't shorts as much as they were the top quarter of proper running tights. Whatever they were, I liked them on her. The designer should be canonized because that sight was a miracle. The long, red, athletic tank she wore intended to serve as a modest cover, but it kept riding up, affording me spectacular peaks of all I wanted to hold tight.

There were at least forty people on the side of the road, dancing and doing the song's matching hand gestures. One man dressed as a cowboy in cutoff denim shorts. The closer we got to the DJ, the louder the music. Electricity charged in the air when we joined the crowd, and vibrations rumbled along the ground. People were wildly gesticulating with their arms, emulating the letters Y-M-C-A: hands in the air, pointing down, then to the left, and finally up to a point above their heads. Amara's enthusiasm was contagious. Soon, we were bouncing while mimicking the letters with our arms.

With each movement, her red tank rose up, down, or to the side, familiarizing me with her toned midsection. Her skin color reminded me of the chocolate Chambord truffles my father bought my mother every Valentine's Day. Just as I wondered whether she tasted as good, the woman herself hip-checked me, pointing to my unmoving arms. Lost in thought, or *lust*, I'd stopped dancing. I liked this silly side of her. We hadn't had time for that back in school, and I wondered what else I didn't know about Amara Grace. It was then I realized that I'd do anything to find out. Before now I hadn't been certain that upon seeing her again, I'd feel the same as I did in school. I did. Something about this woman drew me to her like kids were drawn to an ice cream truck on a sweltering summer afternoon.

By mile three, I felt fine but didn't tell her because I feared she'd run ahead and leave me. I could run but not as fast as Columbia University's track team's closer. That wasn't part of the plan. Just then, Amara noted me walking less tentatively. She suggested we follow a moderately paced run-walk interval leader who passed us on the left to get back to what we should be doing. We did well for a mile. But our easy conversation caused us to get in the path of other racers, slowing our pace and theirs. Not everyone took it in stride. A woman in navy running gear, which had seen better days, sporting a huge white patch of sunblock on her nose, passed us, yelling, "To the right if you can't keep up!" We shook with laughter and moved to the right, where we could walk and talk. Neither of us wanted to end our banter.

I enjoyed how our seamless discourse. After the initial awkwardness, we agreed on things like preferring cities to suburbs, finishing one another's sentences, finding the same things funny, and was surprisingly very comfortable with one another. A runner passed us, turned around, and commenced running backward while vogue dancing and taunting us with. "There are better ways for a hottie couple to get sweaty." We pretended not to hear him until he backed the statement up with, "I know you hear me. I said what I said. You betta vogue," then he spun around with his hands alternately framing his head top and bottom and left and right. Before we could respond, he sprinted down the path.

The Sweet Tea was more than a race. It was *an experience*—one I happily shared with Amara, the perfect excuse to spend a couple of hours alone with her. Well, as alone as we could be in a crowd of 60,000 runners and a few thousand more onlookers. The race route cut north to south, right through the heart of Intown Atlanta. Participants ran on hot asphalt in the middle of the street, over bridges, and through tunnels. In addition to traditional cowbell swinging onlookers, racers were treated to everything from free craft samples from the Beer Dudes to pop-up reflexology massages.

Amara zeroed in on a sweet tea station. Her delight was infectious. "Sweet tea is *not* an electrolyte beverage, and I don't care." She looked adorable peering over the cans as if she were being graded on her choice. "There are so many flavors. I don't know which to get." She walked from the tea booth. "Maybe I should stick with water."

"If that's what you want, but you're *at* the Sweet Tea in Atlanta. Seems like a no-brainer." I flashed an irrepressible smile at a Girl Scout volunteer. "I'll take a peach and a traditional, please."

"Two?" Before she could recite a dissertation on the adverse health effects, I handed Amara both paper shot cups.

"Two for you. Here. Try the authentic flavors before you ruin your palate sampling concoctions. I'm drinking water. You've got traditional Southern sweet tea and Atlanta's best peach sweet tea." Her innocent, no agenda smile returned. *Score!* "What do you think?"

"I've had traditional before. It's good, a bit too good—definitely more sugar than I'm used to in one drink." She sipped the other drink, smelling it, then swishing it around in her mouth like a wine tester. "The peach is nice. I could get used to this."

"Even with all of the sugar?"

"*Despite* the sugar. Come on, let's walk this off." As soon as we returned to the race lane, Amara gasped, "Good, Lord, what's that in front of us?" I followed her bright eyes to the notorious hill. It extended 300 feet long and had a 30-degree incline. Two extra-large booths on either side framed the base. The canopies displayed ATL Hospital logos on all four sides. The tongue-in-cheek message they sent was, *we're here to help before you powered up the big hill.* Blocking the sun with my hand – don't know why I didn't wear a visor – I saw a third booth atop the hill. That seemed more like it.

"Surrender Slope. Didn't you research the route, New York? Seems like something you'd do."

"Clearly not well enough. Let's tackle this monster." Her resilience was admirable, if not overzealous. The temperature had already risen another ten degrees since we started walking. Although it wasn't a mountain, racers dubbed that stretch of road Surrender Slope because by the time you arrived, your body was tired of the race and the heat. The hill exacerbated your fatigue.

3

AMARA

I adjusted my walking form, using my arms to generate momentum. Reflexively, I stood tall rather than leaned forward like the rookies already panting. Hill runs resembled good sex. Your heart, respiration, and perspiration rates increased, and you felt calories melting off you. I wished I could run it. Running burns more energy than walking. Also, it was quicker and had a lower impact on calves and shins. On the positive side, hills were good for ankle flexibility. After today's fall, Jordan needed that. "You can do it, Jordy! Oops, forgot you hate that."

Jordan's face flushed as he looked away from me. "Don't hate it. Plenty call me that."

"So, you just hated me saying it?"

"Hated *how* you uttered it. You were derisive, dismissive, and d…"

I winced, "And derivative?"

"Something like that." Silence. Neither of us spoke other word until we crested the hill. Then and now, Jordan deserved better than scorn.

"Guess I was. Sorry about that."

"Why'd you purposely reduce me in such a childish way?"

"It was about me, not you."

"But why?"

Animatedly waving my hands in frustration, I blabbered, "You had the nerve to be—you walked around with all your swag and…" Before I could finish, he stopped, pointed at me, jabbing his index finger in my personal space.

"You wanted me! Swag?"

Sigh, "Fine. You had big dick energy."

*Dear God, did I say that out loud? That ego inflated grin on his face says I did. Please, ground, open, and swallow me **now**. No? You're going to make me see this humiliation through to the end? Great.*

The smile slowly spreading across his handsome face almost made my humiliation acceptable. His head snapped back, causing those cute twists to tremble, "Say what now?"

"Oh God. How 'bout I call you Jay?" I motioned for him to tread around a couple of women who had stopped and were gabbing in the middle of the street.

"Nice try. But we're not changing the subject. Call me whatever you want as long as you get back to that big dick energy comment," he beamed.

*I don't remember him being **this** flirty. I like it. I like him, at least what I know of him. I can admit that now that I'm single. I should have admitted it back in school. I wonder what would have happened if we'd flirted back then. Get a grip, girl. That's the past. Today, all I can do is catch what he's pitching.*

Stevie Wonder's *As* blasting from the sidelines caught my attention. "I've never seen DJs along a race route. Normally they're only at the start and finish lines."

"Welcome to The A, baby. We put extra sauce on everything." There went that irresistible swag. He'd managed to combine the perfect amount of smooth with nerd. "Whatchu know about dis?"

He began a flirtatious two-step, moving closer to the source of the music.

"Oh, you think I can't dance?"

"I don't know what you can do. All I've seen is you YMCAing. For all I know, that's the extent of your moves."

"I'm supposed to fall for that, take the bait, and dance because you called me out." He kept dancing. After a few seconds, I realized he wasn't going to respond. Gently pushing his chest with all ten of my fingertips, I took his spot. "Move over." I exaggerated Jordan's two-step. That's all he needed.

"This what we doin'?" I watched him slowly spin. Worked hard not to salivate at the sight of the tip of his tongue sticking out between his front teeth. "Keep up, New York."

As if it was possible for him to be more irresistible, the man could roll his hips. He didn't do anything leud, but his flow said everything. The dance started as silly fun and rapidly morphed into a sultry cha-cha. Jordan laced our fingers together as we moved seamlessly to Stevie's soulful serenade. Suddenly, we were wrapped in a cozy bubble. The man made the outside world disappear. He and his easy temperament were the definitions of a destresser.

4

JORDAN

That was the perfect time to come clean. We were vibing on the sidewalk dancefloor. She seemed much more chill than anticipated. "Amara, I need to—"

"How did you know Erwin?" We spoke at the same time. I did not see that question coming. Definitely time to abort the confession, so I answered truthfully. "We're frat." She stopped dancing. "Let's walk."

"Are you an Alpha?" I pledged Alpha Phi Alpha fraternity in college and have been actively involved in its social and service events ever since. I was a man of black and gold to my core.

"You sound surprised?"

"I don't recall seeing you at anything." She may not have seen me, but I saw her. The woman stood out in all environments without being showy; her essence was noticeable.

"What, like the sweetheart ball?"

"Well, yeh." She did that cute, playful thing women did when they wanted to sway you to their side without directly asking. She bit the corner of her bottom lip and glanced at me through long lashes. Darn if it didn't work.

"I was there." Her brows knitted together; I could almost see her searching a mental database of Alpha events. "Don't strain your brain. Erwin had your attention."

"Hmm, I guess I mono-focused on him."

"As a good fiancée should."

Too bad the douche didn't deserve any of her focus. Erwin was a sloppy cheater. I always wanted to ask why he put a ring on it if he hadn't finished sampling his options. The jerk took what he wanted, collected and neglected toys and people. Those were interchangeable for idiots like him. I hated being part of Amara's public diss. I saw her fiancé with other women on the regular.

Erwin was an alpha in more ways than one. The frat name fit him perfectly because he tried hard to be a quintessential alpha male. He took charge and charmed people. That made it easy for him to attract others. It also put off people like me. Although we never discussed it, I'd bet good money, he irritated Amara. He had to. She was Black Girl Magic Swagger personified. She had to peep his flaws.

I wanted to holler whenever I saw Erwin out with a slam piece. None of them compared to what he had locked down. On looks alone, Amara won every time. Frat code had me hemmed up. Not that I would have snitched. That kind of stuff was between the couple, not someone who'd happily creep on an asshole's woman. And Amara was his woman. She had the enormous cushion cut diamond to prove it. The ring was almost as impressive as the woman, making it look good.

It turned out that she didn't need me to tell her. When she suddenly turned cold towards me, I assumed she knew that I knew about her man. The way she froze me out, she acted like *I* cheated on her. Stayed with him and blocked me. That was some BS. Maybe they had an arranged marriage or something like that. Why else would she stay? He was decent looking and had a good job, but New York overflowed with men like that. Whatever the reason, I didn't ask nor stick around to find out. After graduation, I couldn't get out of that city fast enough.

"How's old boy?" I had to know. Was this all for nothing?

Her head dipped as she muttered, "He's gone."

"I wondered how long it took you to kick his cheating ass to the curb. How he'd be out in the open with it was foul." I blurted out, shaking my head in disgust.

After a sharp intake of breath and a stabilizing beat, Amara replied, "Erwin died the summer after graduation – a car accident."

Shit. Shit. Shit. He's dead. He died all those years ago. I was so eager to get on with life at the center I didn't keep up with anyone in New York. Those two years were a means to an end.

She gasped, "He cheated?"

With my eye closed, clenching my fists and jaw, I swore, "Shit."

"How do you know?" she asked with a barely audible, trembling voice.

"I saw him," I admitted.

"So many questions. Where to begin?" Typical of Amara to go directly into analysis mode. No emotional outburst or disbelief; she wanted data. No matter how clinical she appeared, I saw the hurt in her glistening coal eyes.

Rehashing this was not a good idea. Rubbing the back of my neck, I told her, "We shouldn't do this." Runners who passed us, waving to onlookers, provided a surreal backdrop. We were talking about her dead fiancé, and they were celebrating.

"Too late."

My twists felt heavy and tight as I struggled to respond. I tugged at the roots, attempting to alleviate the sensation on my scalp. "I'm sorry. I shouldn't have said anything."

"Again, you're too late. Cat's out the bag now." Her dark eyes blinked in distress as she wrung her hands. Questions tumbled from her mouth, "Are you sure you saw Erwin? When did you see him? Where? With whom? Where was I?"

"Does it matter? Scratch that. Of course, it matters." No matter how much I rubbed and tugged, my twists kept bothering me. "How 'bout this? I'll give you the facts, no salaciousness or opinions. Good?" I decided to keep it dry and straightforward, figuring Ms. Methodical would appreciate that.

She wasn't Ms. Methodical, though. She was *Amara*, a woman who'd just learned that the man she'd planned to marry stepped out on her. Her cheeks quivered as she nodded, "Mmm hmm."

Like ripping off a bandage, I got straight to the point. "More than once, I saw him with women at private parties. He was, um… physically affectionate with them. I never saw the same woman more than once. I re-introduced myself to him the first time, making it clear that I knew you. He invoked frat code. I didn't deal with him after that."

"You didn't tell me either."

"I couldn't."

"Frat code, right," the unmistakable scorn belied her anger. I was the only person available to blame. Messy Erwin left an impossible situation for both of us.

"That and it wasn't my business. Think about it, Amara. We didn't know each other like that. What would I look like snitching on your man like a gossiping bitty?"

"A friend, you would've looked like a friend."

I gently challenged her assertion that we were friends. "Were we friends, though?" Amara and I were classmates. The only times we hung out together were with other students in the program. Sure, we had an unspoken attraction, but we neither acknowledged nor did anything about it. We didn't have a special one-on-one relationship. Even when paired on a project, we spent most of our time in public study rooms discussing class work, not personal topics.

"I guess not." Slumping shoulders and downcasting head made her appear defeated. I would have given anything to remove her deflated look.

"At some point, I assumed you knew everything. You became cold and distant. Figured I deserved to be shut out for being part of Erwin's deception."

"That wasn't it. I didn't know. You saw me almost every day for two years and never even hinted. Let me bounce along like a fool. Now you drop all this in my lap. I don't know what I'm supposed to do with the information. Being angry is anticlimactic. It feels wrong to be upset with a dead person." Picking up the pace with a newly erect posture, the anger resurfaced, "At least you're free of the weight of the secret. Right?"

"Again, I thought you knew. For some time, I assumed it was a secret from you. Guilt found a home in my soul. I don't come from people who harbor secrets. It was new territory for me. Every time I allowed myself to think of it, I felt shame in the depths of my core. Mostly, I hated him for putting me in that position. That's not how I roll. What complicated things is that I knew you didn't deserve his disrespect. You should have been treated better."

Modulating my voice to a gentle tone, I stepped closer to her so that a faster walker in lighted sneakers could pass us. "In my defense, we didn't know each other like that. Yet here we are having this awkward ass conversation, and neither of us did anything wrong." Getting heated wouldn't help my case. So, I took a calming breath. "Amara, I get your dilemma. Hearing this must feel like a second grief."

I felt her nod rather than seeing it. "I will have to sit with this before I can process and deal with it. With him gone, I didn't need to know. It's like I'll grieve for him again. This time, it will be for who I thought Erwin was. Or, who I thought we were." Her voice trailed off as she pondered the magnitude of the discovery.

"Jordan, I thought you and I were friendly, if not friends. Another thing I got wrong." I felt the disappointment radiating from her. That ass, Erwin, haunted her in real time.

"Fair enough. I feel terrible. I shouldn't have let that slip. I assumed that when you said, 'he was gone,'… meant that he was absent from your life, not gone gone. I shouldn't have mentioned it." I screwed that up in the most spectacular way. I couldn't take it back. We'd have to deal with the fallout. Maybe down the line, I'd feel the relief she mentioned. Maybe knowing things weren't picture perfect would help her. It would be easier for her to get over an imperfect dead fiancé than a perfect one no living man could measure up to.

Uncertain, I rubbed my neck from back to front with my thumb and index fingers. "I have an idea. Let's sit with it as you said. That's a lot to unpack on impact. Nothing we can do about the past while we're out in these streets. Right now, we can compare running playlists. What were you listening to before we crashed?" My pathetic attempt at easing the mood earned me a chuckle.

"We didn't crash. You wiped out. I stayed upright." Oddly, I welcomed her edgy tone. It was better than her playing the almost widow mourning a relationship that didn't exist the way she supposed it had. In time, I could help her through that. First, I needed her to trust me. If she wanted me half as much as I jonesed for her, there'd be something to work with.

Don't get ahead of yourself, man. You're not trying to wife her. This is satisfying a curiosity. Although she seems like the type a brother should wife. Ooh, unnecessary, errant thoughts, I vanquish thee. Quick, I need a distraction.

Soon, we came up on Rosie, an older woman walking,

waving, and posing for pictures. I read about her online. Ninety-five-year-old Rosie had conquered all 54 Sweet Teas, even the virtual ones, during the COVID-19 pandemic shutdown. She was a local legend, so I pointed her out to Amara. We talked about what an inspiration Rosie and her active contemporaries were. Easy-flowing conversation reinvigorated us as we continued our journey, searching for interesting sights. Soon, we came upon a different type of elder. Standing on the sidelines, we spotted a priest wearing a collar and shorts. "Hold up. This is a must. Holy water or bust."

"What?"

"Come get blessed, woman." We detoured over to a tall Jesuit priest in a black short-sleeved shirt with matching Bermuda shorts. He sprinkled holy water with a gold-gilded aspergillum and blessed anyone who stopped before him. That was true religion. Bless all, no matter their affiliations and beliefs.

It reminded me of our second year when Easter, Passover, and Ramadan overlapped. Fed up with being students 24/7, someone in our exhausted class got the idea of having an interfaith potluck dinner. All were welcomed. Amara brought a massive container of Ethiopian stew with piles of injera. I remember asking why she didn't bring Jamaican food. She blushed and reported that she didn't have time to cook and couldn't trust randos to do it well, so she ordered from her favorite Ethiopian spot. To make up for what she called *cheating,* she also brought an assortment of African décor to set the mood around her dish.

I contributed two lasagna pans of homemade baked mac-n-cheese. That's been my go-to signature potluck contribution since high school. I remember my chest swelling with pride when she praised my skills.

After the holy water, we sauntered back into the race pack. By this time, we were strolling more than speed walking. "Okay, Ms. Precise. What's in your earbuds?"

"A book."

"A book, different but cool. Which?"

"*The Courage to Be Happy*," her chin jutted out in a defensive pose, yet she didn't break stride.

"Not what I expected." This woman and her big brain. "You can concentrate on that while running?"

"Running is reflexive for me. It doesn't occupy brain space. I don't think about it while I'm doing it. Plus, this is written like a story, a powerful story." Ichiro Kishimi's follow-up to *The Courage To Be Disliked* continued a conversation between a philosopher and a young man. In it, the two uncovered lessons from Alfred Adler's work. No matter how friendly the writing, it contained a lot to distill. Only Amara would consider it light listening for a race.

"What else you got on there?"

"All kinds of things."

I gestured for her to hand over the device. "Let me see."

"No." She deadpanned. We mock-wrestled over her phone. She relinquished it under the duress of tickles. Beads of perspiration dotted her hairline and upper lip. Play fighting in the rising temperature was a fool's game. Yet, it yielded me the spoils and relaxed her.

"I won. Unlock it." The prospect of discovering more about her through her audiobook collection intrigued me. You can tell a lot about someone through the music and books they chose to keep on them. Amara's audiobook app dripped with graphic novels and heavy non-fiction titles. Scrolling down the list, I found a surprise section. "You like fantasy and Afrofuturism!"

"Doesn't everyone?" Sarcasm was cute on her.

"You'd think. *The Fifth Season!* That's my shit. I've read that book three times. N.K. Jemisin is a genius. How she presents Essun, Damaya, and Syenite as different beings is masterful." I could nerd out on Jemisin's work for hours. Most women I'm attracted to and vibe with tolerated that part of me but weren't into it. A few tried. Each time, we eventually agreed that they didn't have to like everything I did and vice versa. But Amara already liked what I liked. She understood my career choice and read the same books.

"Right! Have you read *The Obelisk Gate* and *The Stone Sky*?" Palatable excitement radiated from her.

"Is Hayao Miyazaki the greatest animation director of all time? Of course, I've read them."

"Jemisin and Miyazaki, you're speaking my love language. I adore me some fantasy and Anime. I can't decide whether *Howl's Moving Castle* is over or underrated. I don't care. It's a beautiful movie."

Esquisite, intelligent, and into the same things. I adored this woman and needed to know more about her.

We picked up our walking pace, noting the humorous procession of costumed racers. Heat rose up from the asphalt. Fourth of July in Atlanta and outdoor strenuous activity didn't mix. This year was a testament to that. I felt streams of sweat rolling down my back, and we'd only walked. Amara was equally wet. The fast runners we began with must be drenched. The finishers who doubled back on the route looked dry in their recently earned raced t-shirts, but their shorts were water-logged. They modeled our impending future. Until then, we had a race to finish.

We took silly selfies at mile marker eight. The lines to pose at mile markers got shorter with each mile. The novelty wore off as racers grew increasingly tired. Turned out Amara liked duck-face posing. I didn't, because what CIS straight man did, but I happily struck poses with her. I taught her how to throw up A fingers for Atlanta.

Down the road, she went berserk when a DJ played a reggaeton song. "All right now, Atlanta's got some flavor. If they play dancehall, you may learn something." Dancing under the elevated booth, her winding hips had me in a trance. I didn't understand the words, but the sensuality was universal. All I could think was how much I wanted to hold those hips while I did my own winding. I quickly prayed that a Jamaican DJ would be in the next booth. Dancehall music, plus Amara, plus me, equaled my wet dream come true.

We traversed further along the last portion of the route. By now, the crowd thinned considerably. Atlanta in July was heat stroke weather. I smelled musty, salty sweat dripped from my twists and ran down my face. Some made their way into my mouth. Giant misters oozed water from both sides of the street, helping regulate our body temperatures. They also added more water to my already soaked twists. No luck on the Dancehall music. Instead of another DJ booth, we turned the corner from a central boulevard to a residential street I knew led to Piedmont Park, where the finish line awaited us.

She must have sensed my struggle because Amara raised a terry cloth wristband to wipe the perspiration from my brow. "You need a headband, Mister. And, where's your visor? Here. Take one of these." She handed me the green, yellow, and black wristband she'd just used to stroke my brow. "Time to look like a runner, Jay. The last portion of a race is chock full of photographers. Don't want to get caught looking like the race beat you," she challenged me, picking up her speed and pumping her arms.

She looked like my memaw doing water aerobics in the shallow end of her senior community swimming pool. Except Amara emitted sexuality. When she turned and winked at me, I nearly tripped again. She reached back and placed her palms on my abdomen to steady me. The heat from her hands lit something in me. A part of her body on mine felt right. At the same time, a racer using a squeaky walker passed us. "You gonna let him beat you? Let's do this. Run!"

By this point, I'd do anything she wanted, so I forgot about my sore ankle and sprinted. It wasn't easy to keep up with her. Those long legs of hers ate up the asphalt. She must have been something in her competition days.

Running into Piedmont Park felt amazing. We were treated like conquering warriors. Volunteers hung medals around our necks and handed out bottles of water. Others staffed tables with more water, sports drinks, and snacks. Professional photographers stopped us every few yards. It was heady. I wanted to soak it in but couldn't fully appreciate the scene.

The end of the race meant the end of our conversation. I wasn't ready to let go. Unfortuneatly I hadn't thought past this point. I'd thought about nasty things I wanted to happen but not how to get from the finish line to the promised land. This was my last chance. She couldn't slip through my grasp again.

Think, man. That's right. Eric put me on the list for a tented, private afterparty in the park. I'll invite her to that. Her sponsor credentials probably get her into something more exclusive, but it's worth a try.

"You good?" She nodded. "I'm invited to a private afterparty. Should have food. Want to come?" *Smooth as a young buck at a junior high school dance. She's going to run in the other direction.*

"Okay."

"Really? I mean, cool. Let's see which one of these tents it is. All 189 acres of the park seem to be covered with people, booths, and tents."

Amara giggled in an uncharacteristically girly fashion I'd never heard her do that before. It sounded lighthearted. As she did it, I saw what she must have looked like as a little girl, "189 acres. You know the exact amount."

Sheepishly, I admitted, "Last year, one of my kids did a project on Piedmont Park. I may have gotten into it more than she did. I mean, she got an 'A' so," I shrugged my shoulders.

5

AMARA

The party was held in a large, enclosed tent on the park's far side. It was a surprisingly elegant setup. White cushioned folding chairs were strategically placed along the periphery. Despite the early hour, two full-service, gratis bars anchored the north and south walls. Most people were gathered around the cuisine themed buffet food stations. Glasses clinking and forks scrapping plates echoed off of the canvas walls.

As soon as we entered, people recognized Jordan. He politely spoke with everyone who stopped him, carefully introduced and included me in the discussions. Most exchanges concerned the community center and a special municipal election. I watched him schmooze for fifteen minutes before we secreted to a quiet portion of the tent. We found two chairs tucked behind a tall tripod holding a posterboard listing the party sponsors. He seemed relieved to get off that sore ankle and directed me, "Get something to eat. I'll hold our places. When you return, I'll get my food and our drinks."

Standing in the buffet line, I couldn't help reflecting on Jordan's revelation. Erwin cheated - repeatedly. He had to have had the women privately if he publicly attended with them at parties. Our happily ever after was an illusion. One only I believed. Wow! I accepted that new reality without struggle. As painful as it felt, I easily believed Erwin cheated. I hero worshiped him when we were together. My fiancé was an educated, successful Black man who behaved as if the world owed him all of his desires. He never disrespected me to my face, but he consistently presented as if the world was his. A new device hit the market. He had to have it. A restaurant trended. We were there. He behaved the same with me.

Erwin noticed me in Blue Java Café on Columbia's campus and approached with a purpose. Confident and gorgeous the man had me before he asked me to meet him there the next day. He was smooth. Didn't ask for my number, just a coffee date between classes. A second year M.B.A. student when I was a junior, Erwin never pressured me. However, he pursued me with an intoxicating single-mindedness. He wanted me, therefore, he'd have me, as long as I agreed. Case closed.

Life with him thrilled me. He never said *no* to himself and, by extension, to me. When he proposed, I felt honored that he wanted to build a life with me. That man projected a bigger than life image. Who wouldn't be swept up in him? Towards the end, I had had enough excess except for my engagement ring. I loved that boulder. It sparkled, glittered, and shone like a disco ball. But I began to think we were making a mistake. When Erwin died, I settled on a beautiful image of us, which comforted me. I don't regret that. I loved him. Young and in pain, my mind protected my heart the best way someone in their early 20s can. Preferable to the guilt that crept into my spirit when I remembered how close I came to breaking our engagement. Whenever that happened, I punished myself.

Taneka recognized my anguish and helped me escape my despair, which almost overtook me back then. I grieved him once.

Was I doing it again so quickly after Jordan's bombshell perhaps I mourned the fairy tale Jordan aniallated with one flippant comment?

I got lost in the vaulted tent. At least 200 people were milling around inside. Walking the periphery, holding a plate of miniatures, I carried a ground chicken slider, a pint-sized empanada, fruit balls, and two mini quiches. The spicy aromas had me salivating.

It took me a minute to find Jordan because a tall man in a race shirt and black Adidas running shorts blocked him. Jordan looked uncomfortable. I didn't know what that meant. His friend walked off briskly before I reached them. Jordan stood to take my plate so that I could sit down. He slowly took stock of my body as he rose and gave me chills. Whatever that look was the prelude to, I wanted. For a moment, we were suspended in time. He blinked, handed me my plate, and stalked off, mumbling something about a stupid plan.

This was a nice race party. I said nothing because I wanted more time with Jordan, but my sponsor credentials admitted me to the VIP tent. The invitation promised music, food, drinks, photo booths, and swag. Hopefully, no one from the Mutatio Foundation knew I'd skipped the VIP reception. Who was I kidding? They would note that one of the two Black senior staffers didn't show, especially since they knew I participated in the race. I decided to deal with that later. God willing, I wouldn't have to deal with them for long.

I couldn't identify the host but Jordan told me it was a private party. We were surrounded by a mix of runners and people who came solely for this reception. It was an event unto itself. I meant to ask him about it but got distracted. The man mesmerized me. The way he held my gaze as we spoke entrapped me. The whole tent could have gone up in flames. As long as he looked at me, I wouldn't have moved.

We sipped raspberry sparkling water from cans moist with condensation while balancing untouched plates on our laps. Jordan shared hilarious stories about a destination family wedding he recently attended in Aruba. His light eyes glowed with mirth as he confessed to sophomoric antics he and his cousins crammed into the long weekend. The funniest part was him describing being busted by his parents. *"They actually grounded me. They snatched the brown liquor out of my hand and put me on punishment."* The memory had him stretched out on the chair, laughing up to the sky with tears in his eyes.

His legs extended in front of him, and his neck craned behind, making one long, tempting piece of man. He must have heard my thoughts. Before I could get lost in my lust, he returned to sitting with his elbows on his thighs and trained those seductive eyes on me. "If you didn't know about Erwin, and I hate to bring him up again, but if you didn't know, why did you turn on me? You were always distant, but you seemed to actively dislike me at some point."

That's when I confessed to being pissed he turned down my dream job to lead a summer camp, and I had to enter philanthropy on a lower rung because I didn't get the internship he didn't even want. He apologized and explained that he didn't know I applied. He applied because he was worried his first-choice internship wouldn't be fully funded. When he learned it had been underwritten, he pressed forward to spend his summer in Atlanta.

Back then, I was mortified that he'd been so callous about a prestigious New York City internship that drew applicants from around the globe. I'd coveted that position for years because it held a prominent position on my five-year life blueprint. Yet he managed to secure the mandatory dean recommendation before I could. Or so the dean said. Seemed weird to me. I completed my application and emailed Dean Scoffey the day it went live, but he declared me too late. I didn't bother mentioning that to Jordan. Part of me was afraid to learn it had been rigged. It needed to remain in the past like other things that seemed important back then.

Jordan seemed surprised, explaining that he had attended the camp as a kid and worked there straight out of undergrad. It almost closed when we were competing for summer internships. Of course, Captain Unbothered went on to save the camp and grew it into the organization he currently leads. So, yeah, I felt petty, still harboring ill feelings. But words needed to be expressed.

Jordan began rapidly snapping his fingers. "Hol' up. Didn't you end up at The Ford Foundation?"

"Second choice. You don't get it. You willingly tossed *my dream*."

"Why didn't you apply anyway?" He shrugged as if he found it insignificant. I felt my not-so-buried anger spike.

"The program allotted only one dean recommendation per internship. Without that stamp of approval, an application was incomplete."

"If you say so. I don't remember. Clearly, you do."

The gall. I slid in the chair so my body squared with his. "You treated my dream like prison work detail."

"You survived. Pivoting to Ford didn't hurt you," croaked the man, who was not ambitious enough to understand the magnitude of the situation. I prepared to have it out with him as I should have eight years ago.

"Actually, it did. I had to start further down the ladder at Mutatio than I would have had I followed my plan."

"So, you would have been an even younger, youngest VP at Mutatio?" There he went, tilting his head sideways to look into my eyes. I couldn't be irate while staring into his mesmerizing honey-brown eyes.

I tried not to smile. "Don't do that. Don't show the flaws in my argument. I want to stay mad."

"I don't think you do." His eyes grew darker as he peered at me, and I couldn't look away. Those beautiful eyes offered something more delectable than the goodies on my plate.

Before I willingly got in trouble, my phone buzzed with a text notification that broke the spell. The text didn't help my growing attraction to Jay. Crazy Taneka sent a GIF of the actors playing the Obamas in "Southside With You" with my face on Michelle's body and Jordan's on Barack's. I couldn't delete it fast enough. Lord knows where she found a picture of him. The internet wins again.

"Good news?"

I admitted, "My friend is pathological." Through the tent opening, we saw the crowd dispersing as the sun rose higher in the sky, indicating it was time to leave the park. "This was nice. Thank you for the party and company. I'm glad we got closure on what went down back in school," I mentioned, ending our surreptitious reunion on a good note. I need to return to the hotel and catch up with Taneka."

He stretched his long legs, rotating the tender ankle. "Oh, what are you women up to today?"

"I never know with her. She abandoned me this morning. Who knows if she'll make it out this afternoon."

"Have you had a chance to see the city?" His right leg quickly bounced up and down as he looked past me, unusual since he'd been gazing directly at me. If I didn't know better, I'd have assumed unflappable Jordan was nervous.

"No. I hoped to hit the King Center, Carter Library, and National Center For Civil And Human Rights today."

"Those are must-see spots. Facts. I notice you left out the most important site – Morehouse."

"That's right. You bleed maroon. I hate to tell you, but college visits weren't on my list."

He clutched his heart, affronted, feigning injury. "The House is more than a college. Tell you what. I can give you a quick tour. We'll drive by the highlights. As long as you understand, stopping at Morehouse and Spelman is mandatory. How'd you like to tour my Atlanta?"

I wanted to spend more time with him but couldn't come off thirsty, so I hesitated. "I don't want to put you out."

"You won't be. It's my idea." He lowered, tilted his head under my chin, and peered at me with wide, soft brown eyes. They matched his hair. "It'll be fun." *Were his eyes always this hypnotizing*? I couldn't resist. Not that I would actually break away. In three hours, he had gotten ahold of something in me that now belonged to him. I wasn't complaining.

"Okay," I couldn't stop the smile spreading across my face.

"I got you. First, we have to take a rideshare to my car, and then it's on."

"We're taking a car to your car?"

He stood and stuffed his hands in his pocket, "When you say it like that, it sounds ridiculous." Shaking his head as if remembering something, he held his hands out to help me up from my seat. "We're ride-sharing to my boy Mychal's office building. I parked my car there because it was free and far from race traffic. As much as I love ATL, it does have the worst traffic. Has peeps plotting and planning how to get from point A to point B." He tapped his phone and said, "Car will be here in four minutes. Let's walk to the pick-up zone."

6

JORDAN

The compact electric rideshare car resembled one of those circus clown cars barely big enough to fit a gymnast yet was filled with 72 adult clowns wearing huge floppy shoes. Our driver, Bill, could have been one of those clowns. He had a red bulbous nose, a mostly bald head, and unkept hair around the edges. He assumed we were husband and wife, and I can't lie; I kind of dug it. She didn't jump to correct him, so I went along with the charade. Bozo Bill gave us outdated, heteronormative, paternalistic marital advice. Unfortunately, he drove like a clown. Bruh had us clutching the armrests.

When he asked whether Amara had dinner ready when I returned from work and kept a clean house, her eyes bugged out so far that I thought I'd have to catch and push them back into her head. We cracked up when Bill told her not to be career-driven and that a high school education was plenty for wives. I told him she had a doctorate and worked on world peace, for real, working with people across the globe. He responded, "I'm too late. Maybe you can keep that part of you from home." I asked him if his wife did that. When he admitted to being four times divorced, we laughed so hard that my side hurt. Bill was more of a clown than he appeared.

A three-story downtown building with a modest gated parking lot in the rear housed Mychal's medical office. We attended Morehouse together. After college, he went into commercial real estate management. Since we were scrawny freshmen, he'd been talking about how "God ain't making any more land." I couldn't argue with that. Because of him, each member of our crew owned at least one home. He took it further with a few office buildings and a strip mall he had a majority stake in.

Using the code he gave me to enter, we moved toward the rear of my late-model, unassuming SUV. "I was expecting a Charger, Mr. ATL, the official car of your city." I flashed a sheepish grin. This woman humbled me in more ways than one.

"What's that look for? Oh my, God. You have a Dodge Charger!"

She had my big ass blushing. "Had."

"What happened to it?"

I loved that car. You couldn't tell me a thing when I was behind the wheel. She did right by me for ten years. I'd still be driving her if she hadn't been stolen from in front of a club I shouldn't have been at on a Wednesday night. Taking a cosmic hint, I replaced her with something more befitting a man with a day job. Plus, she didn't have enough room to cart the endless boxes I transported to the center.

"We grew apart."

"Did it have a name?" She full-on teased me. Fun Amara was light years more pleasurable than angry Amara.

"I plead the fifth."

We got in the truck and quietly drove south to Morehouse. I was processing and scheming—processing everything I'd learned about her and scheming to get her alone. Before I knew it, we were pulling up to the college's front gate. "Welcome to the Mecca."

We parked in a multilevel car lot. Distracted by her pulling her shorts legs down I almost didn't hear her quip, "Tell me about this magical place, Jordan."

"Hmm? Oh. Morehouse has been educating Black men for 150 years. It's been turning Black boys into Black men and preparing them to be leaders. Civil rights, business, educational, political leaders, entertainers, and Rhodes scholars are within our ranks. More importantly, The House changes men's lives. The domino effect of that is incalculable." I couldn't hide my pride. "I'll show you a few key sites, including Spelman, Clark, and Morris Brown. Together, we make the Atlantic University Center, otherwise known as HBCU heaven."

"I already know of your sister school, Spelman College, and Clark Atlanta, the largest of the group, but isn't Morris Brown closed?"

"It's coming out of a bad spell, but still here. Can't keep a historically Black College down."

We toured the AU Center. Most buildings were closed for the holiday, but I gave her a feel for the place. Always the intellectual, she was disappointed we couldn't enter the museums and galleries. Showing her my old haunts and significant places, like where I performed my first Alpha step routine, had me giddy. I even told her the secret to sneaking out of Spelman dorms. Something about her made me want to share.

I loved Morehouse and needed her to understand the depth of that, of me. I tried to keep it together when we came upon President Benjamin Mays' statue, which marked his and his wife's, Sadie Gray Mays, graves. That spot always affected me. Being there with Amara made the moment more poignant.

As I showed her around, we spent a lot of time talking about our chosen careers. I was in awe of how she perfectly summed up my approach to life: doing no harm is nice, but we're required to do good. As I pointed out sights like the tapered stone Howard Thurman Obelisk and the bronze statue of Dr. Martin Luther King outside of the Chapel Amara, she confirmed what I suspected—she cared about people.

We watched a group of German tourists frustratingly try to use an app on the Thurman Obelisk. Amara struck up a conversation with them in stilted English. She read the inscriptions to them and found Rev. Thurman's Wikipedia page on one of their cell phones.

Fortunately, the Atlanta University Center school grounds were expansive enough for us to have a wide-ranging exchange as we toured. "Why didn't you stay at Columbia? Why do the MS at the New School? I know Ms. Spreadsheet got into all the programs."

"The New School programs seemed more community-minded. The Columbia one was like an old-school MBA with a concentration in non-profit management. How about you?"

"I moved to New York City for that program. I hear you about ours being more in tune with the grassroots. That's why I chose it." I could have stayed local for graduate school, but the New School's Milano School's non-profit management program was the legendary OG in the field. I was drawn to its combination of progressive thought and real-world practicum. I needed exactly that to take the center to the next level.

I pegged Amara for a more traditional, almost corporate program, but she didn't choose that. The most strait-laced and youngest in our class, she worked hard and produced, proving that first impressions can be misleading.

"Yes! I wanted to get dirty, figuratively."

"Dirty at a philanthropic foundation?"

"You're right, poor word choice. Getting dirty isn't me. But helping is. I learned young that I'm not cut out to be on the front lines of anything. I'm a good student. I can evaluate. Numbers don't scare me. I figured I could match my strengths with a means to work with or help grassroots organizations."

"How did you leap from that self-assessment to professional philanthropy?"

A brilliant smile claimed her face. Right then, I knew I'd do anything to keep it there. "Don't laugh," she warned. "At fourteen, I saw Melinda Gates on *60 Minutes*. I'd never heard of organized giving until then. How she talked about zeroing in on an issue to improve or eradicate a problem lit something in me. I knew rich people donated money, but she did more than throw bills at a problem. She was *part* of the solutions."

Amara punctuated her words with sweeping hand gestures. "How she described funding strategy, research, and working tangentially in the trenches with professionals like you fascinated me." This woman, man. She sounded as passionate about philanthropy as I did about community development. I wanted to pick her up and scream, *It's you*! I played it as cool as possible, considering I'd just fallen a little bit in love with her.

"I know what you mean. We're taking different routes to the same destination. For me, it's comprehensive community development. I live for getting dirty." It had been longer than I liked to admit since I was hands-on at the center. "Well, being closer to it than you. Executive directors don't do direct service. Every day I'm on site, I set aside time to check in with our constituents. I have to keep my fingers on the pulse. Kids and elders aren't shy about telling the truth. And they're fun." How she unabashedly stared at me with her mouth slightly open made me feel like a conquering hero in a kiddie flick. "I'm lucky. Not many people get to play at work. Or hear elders uncover long-buried stories."

I played myself. A brother didn't fall for a lady in hours. I mean, I knew her back in school, but still. I was feeling things for her it took months to have with other women. I couldn't have caught real feelings in half a day. Maybe my brain manufactured emotions because I wanted in her pants. That I'm sure of. Feelings meant a relationship. How would that work? She lived in New York. She'd only ever lived in New York. Her family was there. She had a good job. We could do long distance, but was that sustainable? Despite logic, I couldn't help but ponder what would happen if we nurtured this thing sprouting between us.

Whoa, I'm getting ahead of myself. Slow down, man. Start with figuring out how to spend more time with her today. "You hungry? Because I could eat."

"Me too. We were surrounded by all of that free food in the tent and picked at our plates."

"The conversation was worth the sacrifice." We stared at each other, sharing an unexpressed enigma. "I know the perfect tour stop for lunch."

AMARA

"Welcome to the headquarters of The City Too Busy to Hate. They ran the Civil Rights Movement out of this place." He guided me to a cozy booth by the window and sat opposite me. An appetizing mixture of grease, spies, and sweetness permeated the air.

"Not in church basements throughout the region." I had sarcasm turned on high this afternoon.

"Those too, Smartie. But Pascal's was a special spot. It was a meeting place for entertainers, politicians, and businesspeople. Civil Rights icons, including Dr. Martin Luther King, Jr. and his lieutenants, frequented it."

I didn't play with lunch. I flirtatiously asked the young waiter several questions before deciding on the meal. Coincidentally, Jordan had the same one every time he ate here, which he told me wasn't often enough. Finished with the important business, chin in my hands, elbows on the table, I gave him my full attention. "Tell me more about this place."

"The Paschal Brothers often posted bond for arrested Civil Rights protestors. They also served complimentary meals and extended store hours to provide a central location where parents and friends greeted loved ones after release from jail."

Having a meal with Jordan was nice. Something about soul food gave one permission to be real. We opened up over collards, mac-n-cheese, and catfish. I'd never been shy around food. I ate my mac-n-cheese and his. It didn't taste as good as the one he made for a potluck we had in grad school, but it still hit the spot. All those carbs had me revealing things. Apparently, I didn't need tequila to blab my truth.

"About me being attracted to you. It's true. I liked that you were grown, with lived experiences but not old; a few years makes a difference when dealing with 20-somethings. I despised myself for having those feelings. I felt horrible about it because I was engaged. I'd voluntarily taken myself out of the dating pool and still found it possible to have feelings for another man. It made me sick to my stomach. Literary. One night, I vomited, thinking about my emotional treachery. What a joke that is now."

He leaned in, licking his juicy, full lips, "Do you *still* have those feelings?"

"It's been a while, Jay. I don't know how I feel about much—except my career. I'm clear on that, and I'm crystal clear on the impact I want to make."

"I hear you. I'll table that question and pitch an easier one." The self-satisfied way he leaned back in the booth told me we weren't done with that topic. "What type of relationship do you desire? Don't fix your mouth to lie. I know you've thought about it. You think about everything. You're the most intentional person I've met."

Wistfully, I responded, "I want a good life."

"What does that mean?" He leaned in to hear my response, letting me know he was vested in it. He wanted to know what I had to say. He was so close that I could smell the sweet tea on his breath.

Wiping crumbs from my mouth, I told the truth. "I want a good life with a buddy."

"Buddy?" he chuckled, nearly spitting out the sweet tea he'd sipped from a mason jar.

"Yes. Stop laughing. An active sex life is a given, so hush," I couldn't help but swat him on his broad shoulder, flexing under the blue tank top. "But I'm talking about the real stuff. I want a friend, a buddy to swag through life with. I want inside jokes. Exploring. Hiding from kids. Holding up during tragedy. I want movie nights, couple's retreats, recuperating after weekends filled with kids' activities, and long talks at bedtime." It was the truth. I wanted a life partner. The more items I listed, the more profound my realization that being in a relationship moved further up on my life plan. "What do you want?"

He twirled a few of my temple curls around his index finger, then slowly looked me up and down. Without hesitating, Jordan declared, "To know my woman so well that by her scent, I can tell where she is in her cycle and what type of dick energy she needs."

My gosh! I had nothing except, "That's some serious swag energy, Jay." We stared at one another. Slowly, he trailed an index finger down the bridge of my nose and over my lips and used that same finger to raise my chin closer to his mouth. I was mildly shocked when my phone vibrated with a call. Confused, I fumbled with the device. "Hello."

"Gurrlll, I'm in a crisis."

Still dazed, I had difficulty comprehending T's words through the connection. She sounded

alarmed. "Wha… what happened?"

"My mechanic called, not texted, not DM'd, *called* like we booed up. I think he wants

more."

Taking a deep breath, I shook my head and closed my eyes. *"That's* why you called me

instead of texting?"

"No. I mean, I do want you to know about the stalker mechanic in case I disappear. But I'm calling to find out if I'm going to see your Black ass before you jet back to New York. Or will the rest of your time in Atlanta be spent stocking up on vitamin D, and I don't mean sunshine? Dick. I'm talking about D.I.C.K." Her voice grew increasingly louder with each word.

"I know what you mean, T. Don't count on me tonight. Tomorrow should be good."

"Ooh, you are getting the D!"

"We'll see."

"Get it! Get it! I see you relaxing your boundaries. Amara's gonna get some, Amara's –" By this point, she was excruciatingly loud. I'm sure Jordan heard her.

"Bye."

"Rude." I heard her retort as I giggled and pocketed my phone.

Taneka had a point. I wanted to be with Jordan. But now I felt some type of way about him. It's no secret I could be rigid. Now, I was feeling insecure. Things weren't as I assumed. I'm good with blaming the internship situation on a lack of communication. But Erwin cheated, and Jordan knew. He made a choice not to tell me about Erwin. I don't know how to be comfortable with this new knowledge.

He interrupted my thoughts. "It's about time for me to feed and walk the dog. Plus, these clothes are begging to be retired. I need to shower and change. I can drop you at your hotel and head to my place. Or we can continue the tour. I wait while you change, then show you how real Atlantans live. We're not all in McMansions."

I vowed that I was going to let go. It's now or never. So, I put it out there. "Let's enjoy today together, wherever that takes us." Taneka must be rubbing off on me because I'd never been this forward with a man; never had the opportunity. I met Erwin in college. He quickly became my first and only serious relationship. After he died, I concentrated on my career. There had been men, even sex, but no sparks. Jordan was *all* sparks, a *one man* fireworks show. So yeah, going for what I wanted seemed good. I was ambitious at work. It might as well be in romance, too. Nothing wrong with being in control. I liked control.

8

AMARA

W e drove to the midtown hotel I was staying in for the week. Jordan agreed to wait in the lobby while I showered and changed upstairs. I didn't stay at such upscale places on personal trips, but the Foundation paid this tab. The suite they arranged rivaled the size of my first apartment in Manhattan. Taneka and I shared that place for three years. Idealistic young fools that we were, we thought we had something since most of our windows overlooked a community garden on the west side of the building.

This week's view put that to shame. From my corner suite, I saw the towering buildings of Buckhead in Atlanta and the more colorful tree canopy east of me. Last night, I pulled the beige linen slim arm sofa close to the window and enjoyed the view while I reviewed a white paper my program assistant drafted on the changing global landscape of nuclear security.

I entered the room, congratulating myself on being overprepared. I'd packed a few extra, just in case outfits. Initially, because I never knew what Taneka would get me into. Fortunately, they gave me options for this quick change. What was I changing for?

We didn't discuss what we'd do after he walked the dog. He'd already seen me in next to nothing; actual clothing should not have been an issue. Yet, I stood in front of a backlit full-sized mirror holding a sundress in one hand and a sleeveless jumpsuit in the other; both were black – because real New Yorkers wear black no matter the season.

The jumpsuit showcased my curves without screaming, *This is what I'm offering*. The sundress showed more skin, but it felt more flirty than sexy. What message did I want to send this evening? My magnetic vag was drawn to his iron penis. Yet, I felt awkward about the Erwin stuff. Oddly, learning the truth didn't hurt as much as it could have. The fall from a fantasy didn't feel as terrible as one would think. Probably because it'd been seven years, and Jordan was a nice hard surface to land on. That and, I wanted to find an attractive man with a mind that matched mine more than I needed to hold on to newly discovered, overdue grudges. My phone vibrated with another text before I got too far down that rabbit hole.

> Taneka: Get the D yet?

> Amara: Girl, bye.

> Taneka: String of emojis - smiley face with tongue hanging out, eggplant, peach, rain drops.

Once I slipped into my chosen outfit, I put on the final touches and grabbed my purse, phone, and room key before leaving the room and taking the elevator back down to the lobby. Walking out of the elevator, I spotted his profile across the room. And damn it, I felt butterflies performing an airshow in my stomach.

As I approached, I overheard the tail of a phone conversation. "I'm not thanking you, bruh. That was flagrant." I rounded on him, doing my best supermodel impression. "Gotta go. Peace." I picked the sundress, setting it off with matte red lips, big silver hoops, a snake armlet on my right bicep, and an oversized cocktail ring on my middle, left-hand finger. Fortunately, I'd worn an elegant black band on my ubiquitous Apple Watch. The halter top showed off my toned shoulders and arms. The dress hugged my chest and torso before flaring to just below my knees in a provocative yet modest style. It was universally appropriate, plus, my goods were more accessible in a dress. I knew I'd chosen correctly when Jordan's nose flared and eyelids drooped. We had a winner.

"I see you, beautiful. Ou'chere trying to make a brother salivate. Who made that dress?"

"Why?"

"I want to send them a thank you gift," I blushed and put a little extra switch in my step. Since he liked what I was serving, well, I had more to dish onto his plate.

Once again, we were in his truck. The ride to his house was quick. We jumped on a highway in the business area and exited in a quiet residential zone. The neighborhood was unlike anything I'd seen on TV shows set in Atlanta.

Jordan lived in East Atlanta, formerly the home of the Creek people. After the forcible removal of the Creek, White people acquired land there through the Georgia land lotteries. The neighborhood had gone through a few permutations. It had an edgy yet hip vibe. Instead of the McMansions or urban blight Atlanta was known for, we drove past treelined streets with cute bungalows and craftsman-style homes with landscaped front yards. Many were recently renovated and expanded.

In no time, he turned onto a side street, and the truck slowed to enter the carport of a white with black trim craftsman. Black

Adirondack furniture occupied the wrap-around porch, and well-manicured hedges and shrubs delineated the property lines. It looked like a well-loved home, different from the bachelor pad I expected. "Nice."

"Thanks," he sighed and patted the side of the house. "Wasn't so nice when I bought it."

"You did the renovations?"

"Uh-huh. Put a lot of sweat and actual blood into her. Took forever. But I learned a lot, and it's appreciated more than I imagined." His earned pride was evident. He adorably swayed with both hands in his shorts pockets.

"Oh. You renovated, as in, did the physical labor?"

"Yeh, most of it. Called in pros for the tricky stuff. Too blue collar for you?"

"Leave me." His negative assumption had my don't try me Jamaican attitude rearing its head. "I like what I'm learning about you. I was thinking that's impressive..." *and hot.*

"Thanks. Got lucky. I wanted back in the old hood, but gentrification priced me out."

"You grew up around here?"

He nodded. "Parents live three blocks down and around the corner. The Center is half a mile east."

"Wow. So, how did you snag this place?"

"It was a mess. Investors were offering the owners tons of cash to buy and tear down. I couldn't match that, so I appealed to their "help a brother out" consciousness. I reminded them how it felt when they bought it. Everyone told me I was crazy; she'd been empty for years, but I knew. I knew we belonged together."

I remember this feeling. I always liked how he got lost in a topic. Listening to him go deep into something transfixed me, like the time we were working on a case study of a youth center in The Bronx. Jordan was our in-house expert, schooling us on the difference between legally expected, ethically demanded, and morally dictated. The example he used blew me away. Children's athletic coaches had minimal legal obligations. However, their ethics led them to go beyond those in support of the players. Morals compelled them to skirt the law and ethics to keep children safe. He outlined two personal cases where he had to decide which course of action to take to protect a child. Had it not been for a sympathetic social worker, his chosen one could have cost him his job. He was so animated, sharing the stories, that the hair on our arms tingled with compassion. I wanted to lick the passion emanating from his pores.

As soon as he opened the door, a fury ball of energy jumped on him.

"Hey, sweetheart. Miss me? I've got you." Jordan scooped up a mostly white Jack Russell Terrier. The sweet thing had brown ears and face, except for the white stripe down the middle and brown around the base of her tail. The ball of cuteness gave Jordan sloppy doggy kisses. His lips twitched in amusement.

"Daisy, we have company. Amara, this is Daisy. She belongs to my mother. Notice I said *mother* and not parents. Daisy is the latest in a line of canines, which suddenly appeared when I went to college. Mom vehemently opposed having pets while I was growing up. The moment I left, the woman couldn't be without one. A more sensitive man would be upset by being so easily replaced." Chuckling at his own joke, he continued, "I'm dog-sitting while my parents live their best lives visiting friends in San Diego. Mom thinks the trip is their 45th wedding anniversary celebration. Dad is going to surprise her with a Pacific Coast cruise."

The dog wiggled in his arms. Jordan adjusted her so her nose was pointed in my direction. "Daisy, say hello." He presented her to me. Daisy morphed into Cujo when she growled and bared her teeth.

"Daisy! That's not how we behave. Do it again, and you'll get crate time. Apologize and say hello." I held my fist out to her snowball nose. She begrudgingly sniffed it and then buried her nose in the crook of Jordan's arm. "Sorry. She's usually friendly."

"Has Daisy ever met your…" I stage whispered, "ah hem, female friends?"

Playing along, he tapped his temple with a thick index finger. "Hmm. You may be the first." Yep, the little barker was jealous. She could smell the sexual tension between us and didn't like it. I wasn't mad at her. I wanted to keep him to myself, too. *I feel you, girl.*

"It's okay, Daisy. Take your time warming up to me. A woman can never be too careful." After Jordan returned her to the floor, she circled me once, then strolled to the front door, where she sat staring at us. Daisy wasn't playing about her man. I would have felt unsafe if she weren't the cutest dog I'd ever seen.

"Let me get you something to drink. Red good?" I nodded. A little red wine liquid courage would help me bring T's prediction to fruition. "Make yourself at home. I'll walk and feed her, then give you the grand tour. Come here, Miss Daisy. You know what time it is." Daisy marched over to her man and patiently waited for him to attach her bling leash. I swear that dog smirked at me before they crossed the front door threshold.

He was being funny using the word "grand" but it was applicable. The 2,000-square-foot house was a masterpiece in understated luxury. I could see his personality in each room. Jordan explained how he painstakingly picked colors, tiles, flooring, furniture, and art. It wasn't lavish but felt luxe without being pretentious. He had fantastic taste. The first floor was mostly open, keeping the craftsman's architectural style. The great room had a mid-century modern vibe, which complemented the architecture.

As we toured the first and second floors, I got a better sense of Jordan through the three bedrooms: a primary with an ensuite, a guest bedroom, an office that had equal access to the bathroom between them, bathrooms, a basement with a gym and a massive TV for video games and movies; the first floor housed a sparse dining room, half bathroom, kitchen with breakfast nook and dreamy center island, mudroom with laundry which was off of the carport entrance, and rear sunroom overlooking a small backyard.

My jaw dropped when I spotted the yard's impressive outdoor kitchen and lounge area. A cute, bashful blush colored his face as he bit his lower lip. "Seems redundant, but my boys aren't trekking in and out of the house this way. Once we set up out here, we stay out here."

"You like to entertain?" I easily could imagine a group of men eating and clowning one another out there on ergonomic chaise lounges, recliners, or sitting at the sturdy all-weather farm table.

"I enjoy cooking and like to hang with my people. I don't curate parties or anything like that, but a couple of times a month, a crew is here eating good food and having fun." That comment led to a conversation about our culinary preferences. The entire time he told me about the dishes he liked to cook and how he got into cooking, Daisy stood sentry next to him. The dog was relentless.

Five minutes later, wine goblets in hand, we were seated in the great room on a supple, tan mid-century leather couch. He angled himself in the right corner to face me and admitted, "I've always wanted to ask you something."

"Sounds ominous. Should I be worried?" I teased.

"Naw. Just curious… why did your parents name you Grace Grace? I mean, Amara means Grace, right? And your name is Amara Grace Shaw. So why the repetition?"

"You know what Amara means?"

Sheepishly, he rubbed the back of his neck. "I may have looked it up."

"You researched my name?"

"I wanted to know who I'd spend two years with."

"So, you researched everyone's names?"

"Just you." Awkward silence permeated the atmosphere. Eight years ago, the man thought enough about me to research my name, yet we weren't friends. I didn't know what to do with that information, so I decided to table it for later.

"My parents were being extra. Amara is *grace* in Igbo but *immortal* in Sanskrit. They thought it could be elegant grace to Africans and immortal grace to Indians."

"They were casting you as a goddess?"

I cringed. "Something like that."

"That's heavy." If only he knew how accurate he was. My family's expectations were heavy on a good day. We were free to pursue our lives as long as we soared. Mediocrity wasn't an option.

"That's my family."

"Tell me about them."

"Hmm. Where to start?" The beginning, I suppose. "My parents met during their junior year at Brown University. That's when they began hanging out as friends. They'd met their first year during the Black student orientation. As it happens when you're a minority surrounded by a majority, they knew of each other but didn't know each other until they took the same economic class junior year. They kept up the friendship after college when they both relocated to Brooklyn. They began dating when Dad called Mom and proposed. She squeaked, *'No! But I'll let you take me out.'"* I was babbling, only doing that when I was nervous. I'm seldom nervous. Jordan Harris should not make me anxious.

"Ohh! Seriously?" With his fist blocking his mouth, he laughed.

I'd heard the story so often that it stopped being funny years ago. Jordan brought back the humor. Nodding with a smile, I continued, "They married six months later. A few years after that, they bought a house in Flatbush. That was before regular folk were priced out of Brooklyn. Then they had me and my brother. My mother is a neonatal clinical nurse practitioner at New York-Presbyterian Brooklyn. Daddy teaches environmental science at Medgar Evers College. We're from Brooklyn, not New York City. They can go months without entering Manhattan. My brother works on Wall Street, making obnoxiously rich people sinfully rich."

"I have fifty-eleven questions."

"Fifty what?"

He shrugged adorably. "Sorry. That's an Atlanta phrase." There was that swag again, "Who's older? I remember you saying your pop came from Jamaica. Did your mother too?"

"You remember a lot for someone who didn't like me."

He inched closer to me. "Is that what we're doing? Because I thought we squashed that?"

"You're right. I'm three years older than Adio."

"Audio as in an audiobook or adios as in 'boy bye'?"

"A-D-I-O, as in righteous," his almond-shaped eyes widened, and eyebrows rose as he failed to suppress a laugh. "I know, my parents do too much."

"That wasn't what I was thinking. I see you get deep thought naturally and that those names are a lot to grow into. Is your brother doing as well as you are in living up to his?"

"He makes a lot of money. He's a good man, solid. We bicker over our divergent paths, but we agree the system needs people like him to fund the work you and I do. Of course, one could argue that people like him make our work necessary."

"Thanksgiving table talk must be fun in your house." He huffed out his version of a chuckle, which sounded like a smoldering moan. It had me tingling in long-dormant parts.

"Sunday dinner, not Thanksgiving. Adio and I are cool. We get each other. That's why we can low-key judge one another. It's just how we are." I knew it sounded harsh, but he seemed to get it – get me. High-achieving families often got that way through sheer force and willpower. He understood why I grinded as I did in school. Working hard came naturally to me.

"Anyway, both of my parents are originally from Jamaica. They didn't know one another there. People always ask that. My mother went to Brooklyn Tech. Her family moved to the States after her grandmother died. She was 13 or 14. By then, they had more family here than back home. My father says he landed on the Brown campus directly from The Rock, which is what old heads called Jamaica. Before you ask. Yes. We went to Jamaica a lot. It's a second home to me. However, it's been a minute since I've been." I was babbling again. "Enough about me."

Without taking his gaze off me, he stood, outstretched his hands to me, and commanded, "Alexa, play quiet storm."

"What do you know about that, ol' mon?" Jamaican Amara reappeared. *Oops. Where'd my accent come from? I usually save it for family. Girl, you're too comfortable around this enticing, cool nerd. Calm yourself.*

"Old?" He incredulously asked. I hit a nerve.

"I said what I said."

"And I can do what I can do. Com'ere." We began a slow dance that quickly morphed into a slower grind. "This is the kind of dancing I wanted to do earlier. Those DJs weren't helping my cause." Alicia Keys' *Un-Thinkable* oozed through a hidden Blue-tooth speaker. The perfect song for the moment because my brain and my vag weren't in accord. *But if he ask me, I'm ready.*

For once, I went with Ms. Vag; she was much more fun. Alicia continued to sing. *I deserve it. I know I deserve it.* Despite her triflingness, Taneka spoke the gospel. Ms. Vag had been severely neglected. Standing on my tiptoes, I embraced him tightly and leaned in for a kiss, feeling his touch on my lip. With a playful gesture, I bit his lower lip. I couldn't help but feel the heat radiating from his body. He ran his fingertips up and down my spine, making my heart race with desire. "May I taste your lips, Mara?"

"Hmm."

"I can't hear you. Say it, Grace."

"Y- ye- yes," I stammered as I melted beneath his touch.

We stood there grinding, caressing, and kissing like teenagers getting it in before their rides pulled up after the dance. His fingertips wreaked havoc on my skin, and at the same time, his tongue traced my outer ear and jawline. Shivers and goosebumps followed his every movement.

"I see you like the tip of my tongue. How 'bout I show you what else I can do with it?" His magical tongue traced my lips before moving down my neck. I shook with a profound, resulting shudder. "You like that? Imagine this tip roaming your clit. Now imagine my other tip there." Good Lord! This man wanted to speak me into an orgasm. The more he talked, the harder my nipples became. "Mara, did you work out all your muscles in your track days?" I nodded. That was the second time he'd shortened my name, and I was here for it. It sounded embarrassingly good rolling off his tongue. It sounded almost like *amore* (love in Italian). Ms. Vag clenched each time he uttered it. "Good. Let me feel how those Kegels work."

I swear on all unholy, I teleported when he sunk to his hunches, slid my thong to the side, and slipped two thick fingers in me. He was on a mission under my dress, feathering my inner thighs with soft kisses. I couldn't believe that, anticipating the promised clit play, I was on the verge of combusting, standing in Jordan's living room—no such luck. Daisy started to cry and whine before he could get to the good stuff. When we ignored her, she raised the volume and began barking around the couch on her hind legs. That bitch warned me to back up off of her man.

He looked at the terrier with hooded eyes that queried, *You for real?* With his mouth, he hoarsely commanded, "Alright, girl. Give us some privacy, and I'll sneak you those expensive ass treats Ma rations to you." Daisy barked and burrowed under him on the floor, between my wide-open legs. I was too far gone to care.

Jordan gave her his patent look. It had the same effect on Daisy as it did on me. That side-eye grin would undo me. Whoa. Getting a much-needed tune-up was one thing. Falling for him wasn't allowed. He picked up the dog and walked towards the mud room. As he passed an Echo Show, he noted the time, filled his cheeks with air, and exhaled.

Turning back towards the sofa, Jordan exclaimed, "Damn. I have to be somewhere. Come with?" He didn't have to give me details. Today, I was up for anything with him. The smug look on his face proved he knew it.

While Jordan showered, all I could think of was joining him. I almost did. Daisy must have sensed what I wanted to go down. Suddenly, she insisted on having my attention. I relented and played tummy rubs with the competition.

That's how he found us, me sitting on the floor next to a drowsy, upside-down Daisy. Jordan in street clothes had me feeling things. He wore clay-colored linen trousers with a short-sleeved beige linen-cotton blend sweater. The colors popped against his golden-brown skin. He looked delectable. And he had the nerve to smell good. Suddenly, my nipples tingled, and Ms. Vag pulsated – again.

9

JORDAN

I promised my kids I'd drop by the High Museum Teen Poet Slam and Jam. If it had been any other group of people, I'd have stayed home feasting on Amara but keeping my word to these kids was crucial. Most of them already had two lifetimes worth of disappointments. I was determined to be a consistent presence for them.

How she looked at me when I caught her playing with Daisy told me that earlier in my living room wasn't my last chance with her. She wanted me as much as I wanted her.

We rode comfortably to the museum. She asked me about the event and teens, and I shared a few funny stories. Mostly, we sang along to my chill playlist, which included songs like *Home* by Jorja Smith and Lucky Daye's *Roll Some Mo*. Not everyone appreciated these tunes. Unlike other women, Mara grooved in my passenger seat. I caught her mouthing the words to Robert Glasper's *Back to Love*.

Between the DJ fun and this scene, it was obvious that we had a love of music in common. A man could get used to this—lady in his ride, vibing without a need for words. Letting the music do the talking. Yeah, I liked this. Shit. I'm in over my head.

The Museum was a white postmodern building, designed by Pritzker Prize-winning architects, Richard Meier and Renzo Piano. The sun hanging low behind it gave the building an ephemeral impression. If Atlanta was the jewel of the South, the High was its cultural nexus. Atlantans loved showing it off to New Yorkers to prove that we didn't need to fly up there to visit a world-class museum.

Pulling into the underground parking lot and sauntering around to open the front passenger door, I extended my hand to help her out of the truck. She extended one, then another shapely leg capped in platinum, three-inch wedge sandals. The shoes were sexy and practical, like the woman strutting in them. Holding her hand long after we entered the building, the kids were snickering and pointing. They'd never seen me with a woman.

"Yo! Mr. Harris, is this your lady?"

"Mr. H, you didn't say you were bringing a date!"

"Who's this, Mr. H?"

I spoke with each of them without answering questions about Amara. She was introduced simply as Ms. Shaw. Thirteen teens surrounded us, rapidly firing questions about our relationship and the Sweet Tea race. Amara gave me up when she told them I had fallen and had to walk instead of run, initiating them to tease me. Seizing the opportunity, I casually used my accident as an example of literally picking oneself up and carrying on.

Amara was great with the kids. At one point, I stepped back and admired the show. A short, high-energy boy with a close crop fade, wearing black jeans and an orange T-shirt with blue and orange Jordans, rushed her. "Aye, I hear New York coming out of your mouth. I'm BK."

"Flatbush."

"That's what I'm talking about." The boy pumped his fist in the air while repeatedly bouncing off the balls of his feet. "Help me school 'em on East Coast rap. I keep telling 'em the Dirty South has nothing on us. We invented rap!"

I tried to save her from an ensuing battle. "Chris, give her a break. This isn't her lane."

"Excuse me? I'm from New York. He's right. We invented this lane. You're imitating *us* whenever you wear Timbs and a basketball jersey." With a twinkle in her eyes, she dapped Chris and then got serious with him. "Homie, I'm East Coast 'til the day I die, but the Dirty South has something to say. Their horns and snare rolls are sweet."

"Miss me with that."

"Hear me out. Good music is good music, and rap is the epitome of good music: good rap, not fake commercial mess, or corny rhymes. There's room for all versions of it. I like Jay-Z, Method Man, and Wu-Tang Clan, as well as Master P, Ludacris, and OutKast."

Chris dismissively waving her off didn't deter Amara. "Real talk, Arrested Development's 'Tennessee' changed the game." Chris underestimated her. Classic mistake. With a body like hers and sexism still running rampant, it happened all the time. I remember precisely when our program section learned not to do that.

Amara gave off well-taken care-of, private school, annual family vacation, and princess vibes. A few minutes with her, you had her pegged as the type of woman who hadn't known adversity and couldn't relate to those who had. And she hadn't known financial adversity. But she had heart.

One of our grad school group projects took place in a community drop-in center in Washington Heights. They had this odd mixture of a meal program, showers, clothing exchange, and methadone clinic. On our first day on the case, the director was late meeting us. Most of us busied ourselves with phones in the tiny reception area. Through the glass doors, Amara spotted an unsteady woman with three children clinging to her. We'd all seen the unkempt spectacle. While we returned to our phones, Amara stepped out of the lobby, picked up the youngest child, who proceeded to yak down her back, and held another child's hand while speaking in soothing tones to the harried mother, never flinching.

By the time staff approached, the mother was crying and confiding in Amara. Less than five minutes in the bathroom, our girl reappeared fresh as when she arrived after removing the odorous blouse, giving it to the center to clean and use, and using a broach I couldn't recall her wearing to pin her blazer shut. She looked amazing. There wasn't a trace of the social triage work she'd just performed on instinct. That may be the moment I began measuring all women to her. I didn't realize it then, but Amara had been my perfect woman standard bearer.

Pounding his chest, Chris capitulated, "Arite, arite, you right. As long as they recognize we started it."

"Show nuff. We started the modern version of rap as we know it. But our people have been talking, beating, scatting, and whatnot since the beginning of time." She paused for dramatic effect and winked. "But you're right. East Coast made it better."

"That's what I'm talking about. Can we keep her, Mr. Harris?" I wondered the same. *Can I keep her?*

Smirking, I shook my head and turned to Amara, "On that note, let's check out this exhibit that's got people lining up for hours." Some kids joined us, while others stayed in the reception area.

The Anne Lowe wedding gown exhibit was juxtaposed with

selections from current Black couture designers Amsale Aberra, Mark Ingram, and Madelange Laroche. I intended to use our time there to watch and talk about little-known Black history and how Ms. Anne Lowe's artistry was having a posthumous moment, even if her clients didn't publicly recognize her decades ago.

I prepared to use her story to convey the importance of telling our stories and preserving our history so that it's neither forgotten nor left to interpretation. We did a bit of that, but mostly, I watched Amara point out the artistry and explain why the gowns were fine art deserving a museum home, managing to engage everyone. Wandering attentions were returned to the group with a slight head tilt or shoulder nudge from her, causing her to earn pieces of my heart in those moments.

Before we left, I spoke to the museum's audience development person who organized the event, scheduling a meeting to discuss creating a museum-community center partnership. I intended to call her next week, but stopping her then allowed Amara to see me in action. I had nothing to prove, yet I wanted her to see *me* making moves. She made me want to peacock strut.

The kids were on her, as Daisy had been with me, but I didn't hate it. Watching her vibe with them gave me teen crush feelings. I'd planned to stay longer, but that was before Amara started giving me sly smiles. They were my signals, and getting her alone became my mission. I used being late for dinner as an excuse for us to leave.

Walking out of the museum, we were still holding hands. The contrasting shading of our hands looked as beautiful as the art in the museum. Her slim, dark fingers laced my thicker, light ones. Woven together, our hands resembled the majestic tiger's fur pattern. I brushed my thumb across the back of her hand, thinking of other places on her I wanted to massage.

"Do you like Mediterranean food?" I asked.

"I thought you were making an excuse to leave. You really want to eat?"

"You're not hungry?"

"I am but didn't want to assume."

"You can assume." *Damn, I said that out loud.* "There's a restaurant slash hookah bar across the street. Interested?"

10

JORDAN

I hadn't thought that through. Farrokh was renowned with the trendy crowd. I'm not good with trends. I knew excellent food, and Farrokh had it. Thank goodness, The Force was with us. After waiting twenty minutes at the bar, we were seated in plush purple chairs at a cozy corner table. The restaurant's dim lighting punctuated the sensuous electricity cocooning us all day.

Since we snacked on an assortment of hummus at the bar over cocktails, we ordered entrees as soon as we sat. She chose a spicy chicken kabob, and I selected saffron-flavored lamb chops. The conversation flowed with more talk about balancing careers with self-care and personal finances. We bonded over the unpopular idea that although cancel culture was born of a need for safe spaces, its current iteration didn't leave room for mistakes and second chances. The whole time we looked like bobble head dolls riffing off of one another's pronouncements and agreeing.

"Tell me about your family," Amara asked after sipping water. She claimed she'd hit her limit with a half glass of wine at my place and a fruity cocktail while we waited for our table. I took her word for it since later I needed her sober and able to consent.

I waited for the waiter to set our plates on the table and refresh the water glasses. "My mom manages a public library branch. She went to Spelman and Clark for library sciences. Has a doctorate like you. Father works for Delta Airlines as an aircraft technician, a fancy title for a plane mechanic. He earned an associate degree in Aircraft Maintenance Engineering from City College of San Francisco Federal Aviation Administration certification. Later, he transferred to Purdue, where he majored in Aeronautical Engineering Technology in the Aeronautical Engineering Technology Program in the School of Aviation and Transportation Technology; a mouthful, I know." I chortled.

"I memorized that sentence in second grade. Didn't know what it meant but I could say it. Dad earned a bachelor's but prefers hands-on work. His degree and trunk full of certifications enabled him to transition to a supervisory position. He still goes onto the floor to get his hands as dirty as one can in the computer age."

I expected her to bust my balls on the resumes I'd recited. Instead, she searched my eyes and probed, "Are they as easy-going as you are? Like, are you some cyborg laid-back family always in a Zen state?"

"I wasn't always affable." It came out soft, almost sad. To mask the emotion, I took a forkful of crisp mixed vegetables.

"You were a junior grouch?"

I chuckled. "My older brother was the friendly one. I've always been the nerd."

"What changed?"

"He died." My mouth went dry, but I didn't feel the dread that usually accompanied sharing his story.

"I'm so sorry. We don't have to talk about this."

"It's okay. Thanks. It happened a long time ago - childhood

leukemia. They call it that to soften the blow as if terminal leukemia can be pinpointed on a spectrum, or you could forget the patient is a child." I always became pensive when I recalled those days. "Kyle was the charmer. He liked people and sports. Fit in well in the South. I liked books and tinkering. When he died, my parents were devastated. I responded by being as nice and fun as possible, so they'd be happy."

"Were you happy?" No one had ever asked me that. Everyone had incorrectly assumed I was the proverbial resilient kid except Mr. Willie. He saw my pain and knew that I was not okay. Quickly, I became attached to the center and Mr. Willie. A few months after Kyle passed, I was a lonely 11-year-old living with parents who were in the depths of grief. They tried but had little left for me until they dug themselves out of that hole. I decided to check out the East Atlanta Community Center. I liked going to summer camp there. Gambled that it could be equally as fun during the school year.

I loved my parents, but Mr. Wilie filled in when their emotional reservoir dried out. In retrospect, their sad period, as I named it back then, didn't last long, but I experienced a life-changing familial apocalypse. My brother and best friend suffered and died. Our parents were distraught. At the time, I couldn't identify, let alone articulate, any of this. I learned how while pursuing a bachelor's degree in psychology. I also learned what a blessing God granted me in the secure attachment I had to my parents before the sad period. Things could have been much worse. Together, we survived a tragic season.

From them, I learned to value romantic partnerships. As a result, I brought little drama to mine. My women described me as reliable and trustworthy but never dull. They liked that I was comfortable with intimacy and a decent communicator. I treated each one like my queen. But I sensed something missing in each relationship. I wasn't trying to be picky, but I won't settle. I swore

I'd build and protect a world with her when I found the one. She'd never have to question my commitment.

"Despite my misery, I was hellbent on making others smile. Mr. Willie, the director of the community center, knew better. He saved me. That place saved me."

"That's why you wanted to return home instead of taking the internship," her sorrowful expression rubbed me the wrong way. Although I appreciated being understood, I didn't welcome her pity or guilt.

"Since then, all I've ever wanted was to work there, to help kids like Mr. Willie helped me. As I matured, I realized the center could be more than young me had envisioned. That's why I went to the New School. I needed to equip myself with tools to expand our work, network on a larger scale, and move beyond Mr. Willie's dream."

"Have you?" This woman and her questions had me spilling everything. We weren't supposed to be doing so much talking.

"Step by step, I am. We've progressed from traditional youth development programs to a full-service community center. We have senior programs, a food pantry, and employment training."

"Wow. I'm impressed." I envied the napkin she used to dab around her lips. What fresh weirdness was that? Who was jealous of a napkin?

"Don't be. We're scratching the surface. Ideally, we could reduce the need instead of trying to meet it. That's why we've added employment training. I want to do more of that type of stuff to help lift neighbors out of challenging situations into ones where they care for themselves rather than care for them. Of course, we'll keep the youth development and other assistance programs as long as they're needed."

"I'm speechless. You're doing the thang, man."

We laughed. "So are you, Ms. Grace Grace. I can't do my work without funding partners like you."

"True. I'm not a direct services kind of person. When I discovered philanthropy, it was a no-brainer. I could leverage my skills to help those doing the on-the-ground work."

"You mean to put that big brain to work doing good." She easily possessed the most impressive mind I'd encountered yet acted normal. I'd met my share of geeky women, some incredibly beautiful, but none had Amara's *I could talk to anyone in your family* attitude. I liked that about her when we were in school. Now, she seemed more incredible.

Even her hands were a turn-on. They were soft yet firm, and the skin pulled tight around her long fingers. She didn't have stiletto nails like many women. Hers were athletically short with a sophisticated French manicure. On brand for her, a tiny crystal sparkled on each pinky. She always had a little surprise—something uniquely her. Back in the day, it had been her braids. I fought not to picture those fingers wrapped around my big energy.

These deep feelings weren't the plan. I was in over my head, and there was no place I'd rather be, well, except *in* her.

"Whatever."

"Want to play a game?" A silly game would curb those deep feelings.

"Here, in the restaurant?"

"Let's do a rapid-fire association. We'll take turns naming a category, and each will say the first thing that comes to mind. No deep thinking. Can you manage that?"

"It'll be hard. Methodical me usually needs a spreadsheet and charts before making a decision."

"I'll start." She smiled up at me and then pretended to chew her fingernails. This was going to be good. "Best sport?"

"Futbol."

"Football?"

"Ugh, soccer to you. Yours?"

"Basketball. You know. We have a major-league soccer team. You should--"

"Um, hmm. My turn, together this time."

Well damn! How did she take over already?

"Superman or Batman?"

"Batman," we bellowed flatly.

"Duh, Anime or Manga?"

Was she serious?

"Both." We answered at the same time.

"Sheldon or Urkel?" Somehow, the game went from taking turns to her tossing out categories, and I had to play along. It was her world, and I was happy to be in it.

"Urkel." The third agreement cemented our connection.

Sophisticated, Amara became giddy. "Look at us. We're in sync. Tupac or Biggie?"

"Not touching that." I declined.

"Right! That's a fool's question. It's like Malcolm or Martin and Booker T. or W.E.B.? The debate doesn't allow for the breadth of who we are." She got it without me explaining.

"Exactly. It's akin to declaring we get only one approach to life." We were back to being serious, and I was here for it. All day, we seamlessly switched topics and moods. The conversation never ended, not even when talking with our bodies.

"Like assuming all Black people are a monolith."

"You feel me?"

She reached for my hand, "Yeah, I do." The moment was charged with possibility.

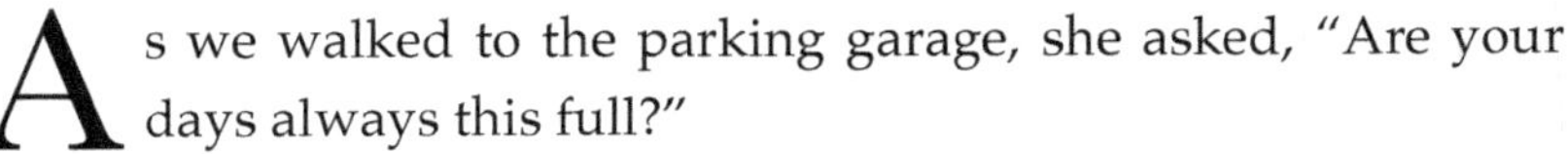

As we walked to the parking garage, she asked, "Are your days always this full?"

"The tour wasn't on my schedule, but I do cram a lot into each day." Might as well put it out there. "I should apologize for dragging you along with me all day, but I'm not sorry. I don't want the day to end. But I get it if you do."

"My hotel is hosting a firework viewing on the roof. Would you like to come with? I understand if you're tired. I just thought--"

"Yes." I jumped to answer before Amara started her flustered babbling thing. I was down for whatever would extend our time together.

11

AMARA

The elevator ride to the hotel's roof was intense. We spent the whole time staring at each other's lips and eyes. The doors opened precisely when I stopped pretending and pulled him in for a kiss. Wrapping his arms around me, our lips barely brushed before we were forced to leave the car. The scene before us had a grown and sexy vibe. "It's nice up here, very chic, like a cross between a sleek cigar bar and an upscale lounge. I like."

All he did was nod. That's not all. He also managed to caress my body with a smoldering look. I felt a warm tingle on each spot he perused. "Wow. Check out this view." I tried distracting him by leading us to the glass-walled edge. "Ohh, there's a spot. Let's grab it."

Pulling Jordan along, I maneuvered us to a partially obscured, voluptuous, white leather, oblong loveseat. The crowd was a diverse mixture of young, monied patrons sprinkled with a few business travelers. The environment gave an exclusive aura. The circulating waitstaff looked straight out of central casting. The one who took our drink orders resembled Armando Cabral. Once our drinks appeared, I managed to calm down and take in our surroundings. Potted trees like those secluding us were clustered throughout. Davido's music oozed from a DJ table. The roof had a stunning 360-degree view over Atlanta. From our nook, we could see nearly half of it. The clear night sky was a perfect fireworks backdrop. Thankfully, the temperature dropped about 15 degrees. I didn't have to worry about my makeup melting down my face. I was so deep in my head that I jumped when he spoke.

"Aren't you curious?" Jordan's voice interrupted my musing. I hadn't noticed that he'd slid closer to me. I turned toward him, resting my head on his shoulder.

"About what?"

"Whether it's more than energy?"

I knew what he meant but couldn't admit it. "Excuse me?"

Smirking, "Do you want to know if I have an *actual* big dick, not just big dick energy?"

He managed to kill and stoke my fire simultaneously. Yanking my head off his shoulder, I commanded, "Stop saying that!"

"Big dick energy! Big dick energy!" he pressed.

"You're a child."

"I'm all man, baby. Come here. I'll prove it." Before I could protest, he pulled me onto his lap so I could modestly sit sidesaddle.

"Cocky much?"

"Literally and figuratively."

I pressed my lips to his, "Shut up." With a hooded stare, he cradled my face in his strong hands. I don't remember who initiated it, but within seconds, we were kissing. We kissed so long and hard we barely breathed. We poured everything into that kiss: our unexpressed desires, regrets, and hopes. It was all I didn't know I needed. I wasn't ready for it to end when he pulled back, panting.

"I need to tell you something."

What now? Just when things were getting good. If he has more nonsense about Erwin, I'm going to scream.

"My ankle is fine. It has been since the third mile. I apologize. I didn't mean to be nefarious. I wanted to be near you for as long as possible. Forgive me?" Jordan rested his forehead on mine.

I felt my shoulders relax. "Thank goodness. You had to be fragile to be nursing a tiny ankle twist that whole time."

He playfully jerked back from me, frowning. "You wound me, my lady. I was seriously injured in service to the crown."

"The crown?"

Kissing the inside of my wrist, he replied, "Yeh. I'm a king searching for a queen."

"A king who serves the crown?"

"Shh."

"Sorry. What kind of queen doth thou desire, Your Highness?"

Cradling me against him, he answered in a lower, huskier voice. "I'm thinking someone in her late 20s to early 30s, a little serious, ambitious, yet earnest. She must be a lean, mean running machine between 5'9" and 5'10" with long chocolate legs that wrap perfectly around my waist as I explore her."

As cute as that was, this conversation train went completely off the rails. I needed to take control, or this man would destroy me in more ways than I wanted. "Hmm. What's your sign, Jay?"

"Huh?'

"Your Highness, this Capricorn is asking your astrological sign?"

"Taurus," Amused, he absent-mindedly twirled a finger in my hair.

"Ah, Taurus goes into Capricorn well. I mean, Taurus and Capricorns are compatible."

He must have caught my gaff because he subtly adjusted his energy carrying member beneath me. "How so?"

"Well, both are reliable and loyal, but where Capricorns are pragmatic and traditional, Taurus is sensual and appreciates simple joys like friends and family cookouts."

"Is that so?"

"Don't get it twisted. Capricorns work hard to please their partners and enjoy being sexually dominant."

"You have my attention."

"I'm just saying."

"Say less." Jordan returned me to my side of the couch, stood, and reached for me. Yet again, we were in sync.

"Shall we take this down to my suite?"

Boom!

The sky lit up in red, white, and blue bursts. There were fireworks over Atlanta and surging between us.

Pop, pop, pop!

12

AMARA

Something about the prospect of us emboldened me. There was no denying our intense connection. I'm not sexually submissive, but in the past, my partners initiated things the first time. Tonight was different; *we* were different. With Jordan, I immediately felt things I usually needed time to work up to. The boldness didn't begin and end with inviting him to my room. As soon as we entered the suite, I kicked off my shoes and pulled him by the collar to the couch, still angled in front of the floor-to-ceiling glass window. He fell onto the blue plush throw pillows, wearing a smirk. Soon, that's all he'd be wearing.

"May I?" I asked, jutting my chin towards his lap.

His tongue darted out to moisten his bottom lip. "Ms. Grace, tonight, you may do with and to me anything you damn well please."

"Anything?"

"Anything."

"Even—"

"Anything." He pointedly looked into my eye and enunciated, "I trust you." Jordan handed me a frightening amount of power. No worries, though. As intrigued as I was with alternate sexual practices, assuming this wasn't a one-off, another time, we'd thoroughly discuss adventurous play before engaging. For now, I wanted more sensual than paraphilic. Doing my best exotic dancer imitation, I sat on his lap, facing him, smoothing my hands over his chest. He grabbed my waist and pulled me in for a kiss, twisting his arms up my back. I paused just shy of his lips. His breath smelled of champagne. "Are you familiar with tantric sex?"

"Vaguely. Isn't that when you don't touch but get real close to one another?" His nose flared as comprehension took root. "Mane, please don't torture me like that."

I couldn't help but smile. "It can be. Relax. There will be all the touching you can handle. I'm thinking of the part of tantric sex, which involves getting to know one another's bodies."

"Now you're talkin', " his relief punctuated the air.

"Ha. Without rushing. I want to learn your body. Awaken sexual energy you didn't know you possessed." His brows rose so high they looked like they were scurrying to his hairline. "Hear me out. Before we get to the good stuff, let's ensure it'll be *great* stuff." I held up my right hand. "Not questioning your skills. If you're willing, let's explore and experiment. The point is to be mindful and present. We can start with eye contact and syncing our breathing."

"Intimacy." He was matter-of-fact about it as if we had discussed the merits of fantasy role-playing games. They fostered players' creativity, self-esteem, communication skills, problem-solving, and leadership development—tantric sex benefited intimacy. Check. Next, I'm into it; him, I'm into him.

"You've got it."

"I want it." That was seductive. He understood intimacy was more than sex, and he wanted it. I aimed to give it to him good. Raising the hem of my sundress, I climbed onto his lap, situating us face to face. I placed my right hand on his heart. He mimicked me by placing his on mine. Good. He was open. I put my left hand on top of his right one, covering my heart. He followed. Then I looked into his beautiful light brown eyes and began intentional deep breathing. Jordan continued to follow me. Once we'd fallen into a natural, simultaneous breathing pattern, I removed my right hand from his heart.

Finally, I could touch those incredible arms. His home gym wasn't for show. The hills and valleys of his muscles were rock-hard. As I massaged both biceps, my breathing sped up. He held my chin between a thumb and index finger. Looked through my eyes to my soul and calmed me.

Next, he gently pushed me back, then crossed his arms to use both of his hands to tug off his sweater. When he finished, he gazed at me again and returned my hand to his heart. I wasn't going to make it through the tantric portion of the night. That one move had me ready to ride him into next week. Instead, I took a calming breath before letting my hands roam free along his torso, arms, and face.

Reaching my fill, I sat back, pulled off my dress, and arched my back. The white strapless teddy I revealed forced a gasp out of his mouth. I smirked as he had before. For amusement, I stood and cat walked back and forth between the couch and window. At one point, I stopped to vogue, prompting him to bark a roar of laughter. I must have gotten lost in my show because when I stopped in front of him, Jordan was buck naked. All those years ago, I thought he had big dick energy. It turned out that's because he packed a delectable big dick. BDE doesn't lie.

I didn't have enough time to fully appreciate the magnificent specimen bobbing before me. Without hesitation, Jordan stood and grabbed my hand. "Come with?" I nodded my consent. We padded to the king-size bed I'd swam alone in for the past few nights. "May I kiss you?"

I nodded. "Kiss and then some. You may kiss, touch, suck, penetrate, and do whatever it takes for me to forget my name."

That earned me a chuckle. "OK, baby. Please tell me if you aren't enjoying something, and I'll find something you like. Otherwise—"

"Otherwise." I don't know who moved first, but we were kissing. There was nothing mindful about our encounter. We were all teeth and tongues until we pulled apart, both breathing heavily. The sensations in my body were intense, a mix of excitement and anticipation.

"Nope. We're going to take our time. Just as you intended. We're not rushing it." He scooped me up and lowered me to the mattress. As he rained tender kisses along my jaw, down my neck, and across the top of both breasts, he husked out, "Your condom or mine?" in the sexiest voice I'd ever heard.

Breathlessly, I responded, "One of each."

"I like how you think," he groaned as he returned to kissing down my body. My heart pounded in my ear in anticipation of the kisses to come. I didn't wait long. He lavished my punani with his tongue, paying particular attention to my clit as he promised when we were in his living room. The man had me under a spell. By the time my orgasm hit, I was delirious. It began in my core and quickly spread throughout my body.

I hadn't noticed him sheathing himself. I definitely witnessed the sun-eclipsing shadow he cast when he leveled his body above mine. Moments before we joined, I heard, "Finally," a barely audible prayer of thanksgiving.

The luxury hotel suite was bathed in a warm, soft glow from the dimly lit lamps strategically placed around the room. Plush pillows and silk sheets adorned the oversized king bed, where our bodies lay entwined in a blissful post-coital embrace. Our view from the floor-to-ceiling windows showcased the twinkling lights of Atlanta, casting a romantic ambiance over us. The warmth of the luxury hotel suite enveloped me as I lay with him. The soothing melody of "Rehab (Winter in Paris)" by Brent Faiyaz filled the room. Its soulful lyrics weaved through the air like a comforting blanket. The song added an extra layer of depth to an already intimate setting.

I gazed at Jordan, admiring how the soft light accentuated his features. His eyes were filled with a mixture of contentment and desire. We shared our thoughts and feelings in those intimate moments. We'd created a safe, tranquil atmosphere. As we lay together in the aftermath of our passion, time stood still. All that mattered was our connection. I'd forever cherish this memory.

"Wow! That was nine years in the making." I exclaimed, unable to contain my joy. After a beat, we both burst out laughing.

This was the perfect time to fill Jordan in. "I have something to tell you." Jordan turned onto his side, facing me. "The Sweet Tea isn't the only reason I'm here. I had a last-round interview for president of the Ngero Foundation." I pasted on a smile and looked slightly past him. "There's a possibility I could be moving here."

"Ngero? The foundation started by Nicholas Folman?

"That's the one."

"What's with the name?"

"Ngero has a few meanings in Asia and Africa, but in this case, they're using the Maori definition – abundant."

"That's deep. Isn't Nicholas Folman officially the richest African American man in the country? The man who single-handedly saved an entire Midwest town by moving not one but three corporate headquarters there, then retrained the workforce for jobs at those companies?"

"Yep. The foundation, not just him. A consortium seeds it. But he's the face. Folman donated half of the initial funds and has agreed to house it gratis in his Atlanta office."

Jordan gently cupped my jaw and pulled my face in so our noses touched. "They'd be lucky to have you. We would." He punctuated the declaration with a sweet peck on my forehead. "Since we're confessing, my ankle not hurting isn't the only thing I should have told you."

I knew this was too good to be true.

"I see you holding your breath. Hear me out," he pleaded. "Our accident wasn't so much an accident as a planned encounter."

"I don't understand. You weren't hurt?" My stomach dropped. What was he confessing?

"Unfortunately, that was real. The guy who tripped me and ran was my boy. I asked him to do that if we saw you. Well, *when* we saw you. I knew you were going to be there. I read the piece the New School did on you. It mentioned where you worked. Later, I read that the lead sponsor, the Mutatio Foundation, required executives to attend. I knew the competitor in you couldn't resist running. You're not the stay in the VIP tent sort when there's a race going on."

That's when I recalled the odd exchange between Jordan and the guy at the after-party. I couldn't hear what they were saying, but Jordan appeared agitated until he saw me. "Your detective work is problematic. Why the over-the-top deception?"

"Baby, I've had it **bad** for you since day one," he held his hand up. "That's an exaggeration. But I was intrigued back in school. After that article, I became obsessed with what could have been if I'd copped to the feelings back in the day. I didn't because you were engaged. Seven years later, a simple photo on my screen brought them back. But I thought you didn't like me. How would

I look calling you out of the blue after seven years when you didn't like me?"

"This doesn't make sense. I didn't like you, and you thought scheming would fix that. Jay, you're too smart for that." Her skeptical look crushed me. I had to fix this now, or the whole day would have been for nothing.

"It wasn't like I said, *'Let me devise an evil plot to fool Amara.'* The idea formed over time in bits and pieces. The whole thing started when I told Joe I aspired to run the race to prove something to my kids and maybe to bump into you."

He got up and began pacing the length of the bed. His nakedness distracted me. How could I concentrate on his words when the big dick swayed a few feet in front of me? I sat up with the sheet pulled up to my chest. Hoping the new position would help me pay attention.

"I can't even recall who came up with the idea. The next thing I knew, we contrived a scenario with an *actual* bump. He wasn't supposed to trip and hurt me. We agreed he'd nudge me into you and that we should keep going. I promise I'd have left you alone if you didn't want to talk."

"Y… yo… you knew I would be here. We could have made plans to run together. You didn't have to contrive a meeting." I shook my head in disbelief. It was all an unnecessary rouse.

"I thought you didn't like me. Remember?"

I didn't know what to think. Clenching my jaw, I saw Jordan with fresh eyes as he petitioned me. "Baby, we wouldn't have talked so long if we had run the race. Quiet as it's kept, we both know I wouldn't have maintained pace with you." We chuckled at the truth in that statement. He pulled out the big guns with flattery and subsequent panty-dropping chin tilt. "Forgive me?"

*Did I? Could I? How did I know he wasn't a pathological liar? My gut encouraged me to **try**. But it couldn't be trusted. The same gut* *failed to warn me about Erwin. All day, I've been going with the flow. Stepping out of my comfort zone. I might as well take it a step further.*

"Yes, but no more deceptions. This has been a lot. First Erwin, then your ankle, and now the setup. I need total transparency. A hint of dishonesty, and it'll be more than seven years before we see each other again. "

"I hear you. You're right. None of that was acceptable. Well, we'll have to agree to disagree about ol' boy. The rest is on me. To be clear, it's not all on me." I gave him a questioning look. "Were you going to tell me you're moving here?"

He got me. I'd withheld the prospect of the job and move, even when discussing careers and

next moves. I wasn't being diabolical. I didn't have anything to tell yet. "It's not a done deal."

He wiped a tear I hadn't felt drop from my eye. "It is. You'll get what you deserve. It's on your life plan. They aren't stupid. Plus, you want to be closer to this big dick energy."

Oh my God! Why did I admit that? I clenched my jaws and shook my fists at him. "I'm revoking your privilege to use that phrase."

"Aye, you can't revoke something you never had the right to. Because I'm chivalrous, if you present an acceptable alternative, I'll yield the privilege," he conceded.

"Hmm. You're too smart for my own good." Feigning annoyance, I playfully pouted, "Umm. Swagger."

"I can work with big dick swagger."

Narrowing my eyes at him, I played along. "I see what you did there. No. Simply, swagger. That's what I mean."

"Boring. Try again."

Chewing my bottom lip, I inclined my head in thought. When it came to me, I snapped my fingers and announced, "Blerd swagger!"

"Unimaginative. Do better."

"It's perfect. A blerd is a Black nerd. That's you, a Black nerd with swag."

"I know what it means—been hearing it my whole life. Admit it. You can't top big dick –"

He'd done it. Issuing a challenge guaranteed I'd step up. "Star-spangled swagger!" We collapsed onto the bed laughing.

"I'll accept it, but only because today is the Fourth of July. And, because Jose Feliciano and Jimi Hendrix owned that song. Otherwise, I'd require something about Juneteenth."

"Marvin Gaye and Whitney Houston put soul on the Star-Spangled Banner." His enthusiastic nod and shoulder roll confirmed that I'd found someone with whom I could have endless obscure conversations. This reminded me of the phrase, heaven on earth.

"I'm so glad Taneka bailed on me."

It frightened me how easily I confided in Jordan. I told him my reservations about the job situation. He didn't try to sway me; he listened. He asked thought-provoking questions and let me know he believed in me. We fit together. Even our careers complimented one another. Every person should have someone like that in their life—someone who got you, someone who wanted you, someone you believed in as much as they believed in you. I needed to convince myself we were that person for one another. It was time to veer off of Amara's aggressive life plan. Jordan may be unexpected, but that didn't mean I had to run from him. Maybe this could work as long as we were open and honest.

Take a deep breath, Amara. It's okay to be a little confused. Don't let that paralyze you. Embrace the happy. You deserve it.

13

JORDAN

While bathing in our afterglow, I decided I didn't care about distance. I may be pussy whipped after one, okay, two rounds, but I wasn't letting her go. I knew in my heart I'd just had my last first time with a woman. Amara was everything I wanted and things I didn't know existed. We were destined for this relationship. Ignoring our attraction in school may have been the right choice then, but the pull wouldn't be denied now. We'd figure things out along the way.

Believe it or not, we already had an emotional attachment. Sexual chemistry and intellectual compatibility, I understood, but *the emotions* caught me off guard. I was okay with that. Throughout the last few hours, Amara and I had explored many topics, yet we avoided discussing the one thing that would bring peace to my heart. Our bond had strengthened quickly as we got to know each other, but we hadn't broached the subject of our future. Now that we'd both come clean, no more secrets were hidden in the shadows.

I had a clear vision of what I desired: Amara. I wanted her to choose me, cherish me, and nurture our blossoming romance into something beautiful. The challenge lay in expressing my feelings to her without imposing pressure or expectations.

EPILOGUE
AMARA ~ OCTOBER

I did it! Finally, I moved out of the corporate apartment and into my place. Adio was no joke driving that rental truck here from New York. He brought everything I didn't trust with movers. My brother came through. He dropped off my stuff, helped me get organized, and then bounced, claiming to know someone here. I mean, most Black people do, but he looked suspicious. Whatever. I had another helper.

"Daisy says hello."

"Your bitch does not."

"True dat." Jordan exaggeratively looked around the living room. "It's not East Atlanta, but it'll do."

"Shut up. This is cute. It's on The Beltline. I can walk to stores, restaurants, and parks. It reminds me of Brooklyn. And I have an option to buy. It's perfect." I rented a townhouse half a block from the Atlanta Eastside Beltline trail. The Beltline consisted of 22 miles of old, unused railroad tracks that circled the city's inner core. The urban reclamation project contained green space, athletic fields, stores, restaurants, offices, etc. It reminded me of the New York Highline. I liked that I could walk and bike on it.

I seriously considered buying the townhouse. Having a mortgage would be a lower monthly payment than this rent. The house was cute. With three bedrooms, a bonus loft, and a modest finished basement, it had plenty of space for my family, who promised to visit often. I loved that my terrace overlooked a community garden, giving me Zen vibes.

"Too far."

"We're a ten-minute drive apart. Stop whining. You're here to work."

"Yes, ma'am." Seamlessly, we worked side-by-side, opening the boxes Adio brought. Jordan teased me about having a color-coated spreadsheet listing where everything belonged.

I laughed. "Guess you don't want to see the decor placement etchings."

Hours passed as we talked about everything and nothing, with East Coast and Southern rap in the background—more East Coast, though, because it was my house. I looked up from organizing my jewelry chest as Jordan passed me a water bottle. We sat in silence, drinking and thinking. It felt right. I exhaled, "Now I know."

"Know what?"

"What it means when they say your life can change in just one day."

THE END

THANK YOU!

KAMYRA

Dear Reader,

Thank you for taking the time to read Amara and Jordan's story. I hope you enjoyed it. I'd love to hear from you. If you enjoyed *Star-Spangled Swagger*, please tell a friend, post a review, or email me. Believe the hype. Reviews help writers.

Whew! Robbi Renee's Just Write Collaborative boot camp life was for real ones. Drafting a novella in two months and editing that draft in a couple of weeks is not for the weak. This adventure didn't leave time for second-guessing. It also denied us the magical land of revisions, where nice enough stories become good books. Because of this, our cohort quickly became a writer's sisterhood forged in *"What have I gotten myself into"* solidarity. I'm sharing the fruits of that labor with you.

Next up is a story I began and set down long ago. Let's keep in touch so that you'll know when it's ready for you. QR code for website

Thank you for your support. As we say in Atlanta, *I appreciate you.*

PS:

Are you trying to remember the songs referenced in the book? Here they are:

"As"- Stevie Wonder

"Back To Love"- Robert Glasper

"Dami Duro" - Davido

"Home"- Jorja Smith

"Rehab (Winer in Paris)- Brent Faiyza

"Roll Some Mor"- Lucky Daye

Star-Spangled Banner" - versions by Jose Feliciano, Marvin Gaye, Jimi Hendrix, and Whitney Houston

"Un-Thinkable"- Alicia Keys

"YMCA"- The Village People

PPS:

I'm not done. Please read the series. Each book is unique and has a different level of fireworks. Seduction In Red, White, And Blue Series:

- Fire & Ice by Robbi Renee ~ *coming soon*
- Freedom Is Mine by M.K. Seven
- Ignited On The Fourth by Cadence James
- Now & Forever Free by Subira Miles
- Smoldering Embers Still Burn by Elle Robs
- Sparks In The Moment by Juri Hines
- Star-Spangled Swagger by Kamyra Harding

ABOUT THE AUTHOR

Kamyra has always had a deep love for reading and storytelling in all forms - books, movies, plays, and her vivid imagination. Her favorite academic period in elementary school was creative writing, where she let her imagination run wild. As she got older, she stopped writing fiction, but the stories never stopped coming. Now, Kamyra channels her creativity and humor into sharing her unique insights on marriage, raising children, and the struggles of trying to get everything right.

She has contributed to books like *Mom's Night Out: Even Inmates Get Time Off for Good Behavior* and *The Parenting Odyssey: Trials, Treasures, And Triumphs Of Parenting In A Pandemic*, which became a #1 bestseller on Amazon and won the 2022 International Book Award. Kamyra's *Eavesdropping* books are a delightfully fun collection of overheard conversations.

CONNECT WITH KAMYRA

Kamyra is very social. Kidding. She's an introvert who overuses social media. You can find her at:

ACKNOWLEDGMENTS

Praise God from whom all blessings flow. I hadn't planned this book, but I am grateful to Robbi Renee for coming up with the idea for the Just Write Collaborative. She and her team provided the necessary assistance and motivation that allowed me to bring a book from the conceptual stage to a published piece of work.

I am thankful for my sister *Just Write Collaborative* members, who welcomed me with open arms as a new author. To those reading this, I am genuinely grateful for your continued support and for believing in me enough to read through this project.

I have my mother to thank for my love of reading and my father for instilling the belief that I can do anything if I work hard. I am at a loss for words to adequately thank my family, particularly my husband and sons, who unconditionally support my endeavors and cheer me on as if I had just a clutch game-winning three-pointer at the buzzer - in OT.